365

Ways to Say Good Night

By Susan Ring
Illustrated by Sally Vitsky

Dutton Children's Books
New York

Easel assembly instructions:

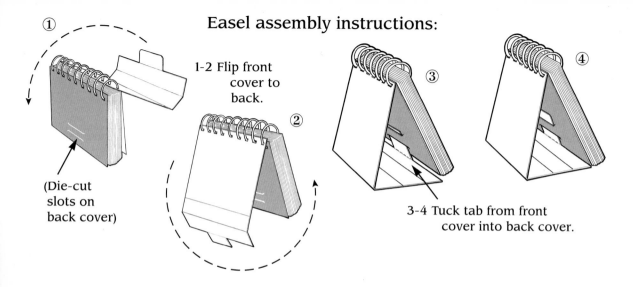

①

1-2 Flip front cover to back.

②

(Die-cut slots on back cover)

③

④

3-4 Tuck tab from front cover into back cover.

Published by Dutton Children's Books, a member of Penguin Putnam Inc., 375 Hudson Street, New York, New York 10014.

Printed in China   1 3 5 7 9 10 8 6 4 2   ISBN 0-525-45956-1

The Man in the Moon

The man in the moon
Looked out of the moon,
And this is what he said:
"Tis time that, now I'm getting up,
All children went to bed."

365

To Holly, for her wonderful ideas, Jill, for her inspiration, and Strider, who gave me 4,105 days of joy.

— S. R.

To Matthew and Alex, for keeping their rooms straight, and to Philip, for understanding why ours isn't.

— S. V.

To Lee, Jim, Jessica, Alexis, Andrea, Rick, Pat, and especially Denise, who made this happen. A special thanks to Christopher, Karen, Joan, and Bill for giving us this opportunity. And finally to R & Z, our inspiration.

— S. K.

Teacher

Teachers are very important people in the community. They are trained to help children learn how to read books, draw pictures, count, play an instrument, and much more. Teachers learn from other teachers, too. You will meet many different teachers as you go through school. Maybe you will be a teacher someday.

364

*F*ew things are more precious to children than that quiet time they share with parents just before bed. This unique collection offers a year's worth of poems, rhymes, story starters, facts, and more, designed to help busy families wind down together. Many of the entries will spark discussion and raise questions. Parents can use this time to explore a variety of subjects in a most relaxed setting. Your local library or bookstore are great places to find out more about the topics that are of particular interest to your child.

Pleasant dreams!

Sandman

Did you ever wake up in the morning and feel dry, sandy stuff in the corners of your eyes? People have often wondered how it gets there. There are many western European folktales about a character called the sandman, who makes children sleepy by gently sprinkling sand in their eyes at bedtime. When you wake up tomorrow, check around your eyes to see if the sandman came to visit you.

363

How Do You Say "Good Night"?

All over the world, people say good night—but they say it in different ways. The French say *"bonne nuit"* (buhn nwee). Italians say *"buona notte"* (bwoh-nah noht-tay). Germans say *"gute nacht"* (goo-teh nahkht). In Swahili, good night is *"la la salama."* What is your favorite way to say good night?

Tree Shadows

All hushed the trees are waiting
On tiptoe for the sight
Of moonrise shedding splendor
Across the dusk of night.
Ah, now the moon is risen
And lo, without a sound
The trees all write their welcome
Far along the ground.

Koala

Koala bears always look sleepy, and they are! Koalas spend almost their whole lives sleeping in the trees. They'll snooze about eighteen hours a day. The rest of the time, they're eating eucalyptus leaves, their favorite food. The leaves have a chemical in them that makes the koalas feel sleepy.

Honey Fungus

Have you ever seen a mushroom that glows in the dark? There is one, which grows on and inside rotting logs. It has a sweet name—honey fungus! At night, the honey fungus has a soft green glow.

It's Always Night Somewhere

When you are getting ready to go to bed, people who live in other parts of the world, such as Japan, are just waking up. Because the Earth turns around, or rotates, as it orbits the sun, it's always night somewhere and it's always day somewhere else. Next time you are playing outside in the afternoon, you'll know that somewhere else on Earth, children are saying good night.

3

The Names of Storms

Storms that occur over the Earth's warm oceans are called tropical storms. People have been naming storms for centuries, to distinguish one storm from another. Weather experts name a tropical storm when its winds reach thirty-nine miles per hour. They use both boys' and girls' names. The name of the first storm every season begins with the letter *A*. Storm names go through the alphabet, but skip the letters *Q, U, X, Y* and *Z*.

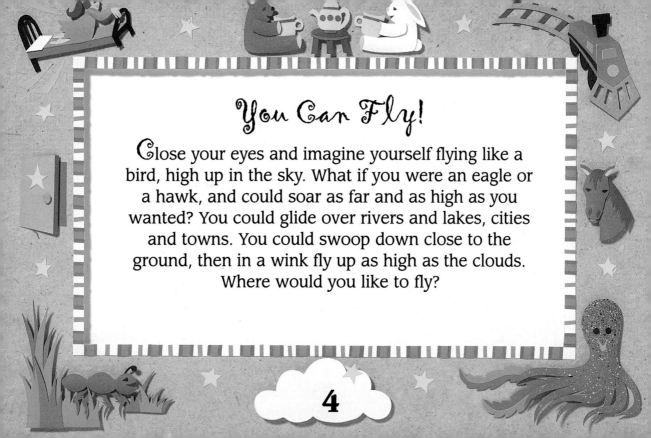

You Can Fly!

Close your eyes and imagine yourself flying like a bird, high up in the sky. What if you were an eagle or a hawk, and could soar as far and as high as you wanted? You could glide over rivers and lakes, cities and towns. You could swoop down close to the ground, then in a wink fly up as high as the clouds. Where would you like to fly?

4

First Flashlight

The first flashlight was a lit bulb inside a flowerpot! Inventor Joshua Lionel Cowen created it, calling it the electric flowerpot. Another inventor, Conrad Hubert, took the light out of the pot and developed it into the first flashlight. Today, flashlights are handy in many ways—for looking in closets, basements, and other places where there is little light, or for finding the way along a path in a forest at night.

359

The Zodiac

The zodiac is a group of twelve signs that represent twelve constellations in the night sky. The planets always seem to travel across the background of these constellations. Long ago, people studied the way the stars and planets lined up or moved in space. They believed the patterns they made influenced people and events. Studying the stars of the zodiac to predict the future is called astrology. Although it's not scientific, it's fun to use astrology to try to learn more about who you are and what your future might be!

5

Draco
(The Dragon)

Best seen from late May to early November, Draco is the constellation of the mythical dragon.
You can see why people long ago saw a dragon in this pattern of stars. They twist and turn just like the shape of a dragon with its long tail.

Wayne Gretzky

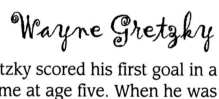

Wayne Gretzky scored his first goal in a Little League hockey game at age five. When he was just eleven years old, he scored fifty goals in one weekend! Now Wayne plays for the New York Rangers. He is nicknamed the Great One, and is thought by many to be the greatest hockey player of all time.

Cat

All cats, from tigers to house cats, are nocturnal. It is natural for cats to be awake and hunting during the night. They have excellent hearing, eyes that can see well in very dim light, and long whiskers that help guide them through even the narrowest spaces in the dark. Although they are tame, house cats act like their wild cousins in many ways. One of the things cats like to do is sleep—sometimes up to eighteen hours a day!

Sleeping Bag

It's fun to sleep in a sleeping bag. Just slide in and zip the bag closed all the way around you. Only your head pokes out, and you can look up and see the stars when you camp out. Best of all, a sleeping bag keeps you toasty warm all over.

7

A Fabulous Feast

Tonight was Denise's turn to cook—for all fifteen
of her brothers and sisters. "I want hamburgers!" the
oldest brother cried. "I want pudding!" the littlest sister
insisted. Suddenly, each sibling was jumping up and
down and yelling out his or her favorite food.
Denise waved her arms and cried, "But I can't cook
everything!" Then, she came up with a plan.
What do *you* think happened next?

356

Moony Names

The moon has many different names around the world. The Italians call the moon *luna,* the Dutch call it *maan*. In the Hungarian language it's called *hold*, and in French it's *lune*. You can even make up your own word for the moon. No matter what it's called, it's the same moon, shining down on the Earth.

8

Hands and Feet Asleep

Your hands and feet don't really fall asleep on their own, but sometimes it feels as if they do! When you curl up on your side and rest your head on your arm, for example, it may start to feel numb. The weight of your body isn't allowing enough blood to get to the nerves in your arm. But as soon as you change position, your arm and hand tingle as the amount of blood circulating to the area is increased.

355

Veterinarian

What do you call a doctor who takes care of animals? A veterinarian. A vet helps baby animals when they're born, tends to sick animals in zoos, and even takes care of dolphins and whales at an aquarium. Some vets take care of pets you might have at home, like dogs or cats. Other vets take care of large farm animals such as horses and cows.

Glow in the Dark

You may have seen toys and stickers that glow in the dark. What you may not know is that glow-in-the-dark objects have been around for more than three hundred years! A chemist living in Italy was looking for a way to turn cheap iron into a more valuable metal, gold. He wasn't able to do this, but by accident he invented a material that made things glow in the dark.

Wayne Gretzky

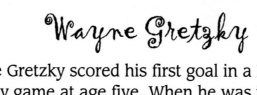

Wayne Gretzky scored his first goal in a Little League hockey game at age five. When he was just eleven years old, he scored fifty goals in one weekend! Now Wayne plays for the New York Rangers. He is nicknamed the Great One, and is thought by many to be the greatest hockey player of all time.

6

Cat

All cats, from tigers to house cats, are nocturnal. It is natural for cats to be awake and hunting during the night. They have excellent hearing, eyes that can see well in very dim light, and long whiskers that help guide them through even the narrowest spaces in the dark. Although they are tame, house cats act like their wild cousins in many ways. One of the things cats like to do is sleep— sometimes up to eighteen hours a day!

357

Sleeping Bag

It's fun to sleep in a sleeping bag. Just slide in and zip the bag closed all the way around you. Only your head pokes out, and you can look up and see the stars when you camp out. Best of all, a sleeping bag keeps you toasty warm all over.

A Fabulous Feast

Tonight was Denise's turn to cook—for all fifteen of her brothers and sisters. "I want hamburgers!" the oldest brother cried. "I want pudding!" the littlest sister insisted. Suddenly, each sibling was jumping up and down and yelling out his or her favorite food. Denise waved her arms and cried, "But I can't cook *everything!*" Then, she came up with a plan. What do *you* think happened next?

Moony Names

The moon has many different names around the world. The Italians call the moon *luna,* the Dutch call it *maan*. In the Hungarian language it's called *hold*, and in French it's *lune.* You can even make up your own word for the moon. No matter what it's called, it's the same moon, shining down on the Earth.

8

Hands and Feet Asleep

Your hands and feet don't really fall asleep on their own, but sometimes it feels as if they do! When you curl up on your side and rest your head on your arm, for example, it may start to feel numb. The weight of your body isn't allowing enough blood to get to the nerves in your arm. But as soon as you change position, your arm and hand tingle as the amount of blood circulating to the area is increased.

355

Veterinarian

What do you call a doctor who takes care of animals? A veterinarian. A vet helps baby animals when they're born, tends to sick animals in zoos, and even takes care of dolphins and whales at an aquarium. Some vets take care of pets you might have at home, like dogs or cats. Other vets take care of large farm animals such as horses and cows.

9

Glow in the Dark

You may have seen toys and stickers that glow in the dark. What you may not know is that glow-in-the-dark objects have been around for more than three hundred years! A chemist living in Italy was looking for a way to turn cheap iron into a more valuable metal, gold. He wasn't able to do this, but by accident he invented a material that made things glow in the dark.

354

The Sun

The sun is not a planet, but a big, brilliant star. It's made up of burning gases that are very hot! Every living thing on Earth needs the sun's heat and light. From far, far away in space, the sun looks like just another star. Do you suppose that the stars, far out in space, might actually be suns, too, and have planets orbiting them?

10

Dirty, Clean

Dirty, clean, dirty, clean,
Can't make up my mind.
Dirty, clean, dirty, clean,
It happens all the time.

I like to be out playing,
But I get dirty now and then.
So rub-a-dub, I'm in the tub,
It's bath time once again.

After that, I'm squeaky clean
From my head down to my toes.
But tomorrow you'll see dirt again,
On me and on my clothes.

Dirty, clean, dirty, clean,
Can't make up my mind.
Dirty, clean, dirty, clean,
It happens all the time.

I Love Bedtime

When bedtime comes, I push away the time to say good night.
I'm really not too pleasant, and I put up such a fight.

But no one really knows that it's just a game, you see,
'Cause once I'm in my bed, there's no place I'd rather be.

How I love to snuggle in with my stuffed animals around
And listen to the crickets chirping their familiar sound.

But please don't say to anyone that going to bed is great,
'Cause I'm still going to try my best to get to stay up late.

11

Space Dog

Can you picture a dog as a passenger in a spacecraft? That's what the little Russian dog, Laika, was when she was sent up in a rocket in 1957. Laika was the very first living creature sent into space. Scientists monitored her health throughout her journey to determine if space travel would be safe for humans. Her mission paved the way for all the space travelers who followed.

352

Yo-Yo

The first yo-yo, a spool on a string, was invented 2,500 years ago in China. It later became popular in Europe. The English called it a quiz, because of the sound it makes as it unwinds on its string. People in the Philippines first used yo-yos to hunt animals. In 1929, American inventor Donald Duncan saw a Filipino boy playing with a yo-yo and was inspired to create the toy.

12

Factory Worker

People who work in factories might build cars, put together television sets, or even pack cookies. Factory workers take turns, or shifts, doing different jobs at different times. Some work during the day and go home in the evening. But since many factories are open all night long, others start their work in the evening and work all night. They go home in the morning. They might be having dinner when you're eating breakfast!

351

Sleep Repair

No one really knows for sure why all living things need sleep, or rest. But scientists do know that sleep is an important time during which the body repairs itself. You may have noticed that when you're sick or not feeling well, you feel better after getting some rest. Sleep speeds healing and recharges us, giving us the energy we need for the next day.

Dark Side of the Moon

The moon orbits the Earth. Did you know that when you see the moon, you always see just one side of it? The same surface of the moon is always facing Earth. Only astronauts have ever seen the other side of the moon.

350

The Gift

It was Ivy's seventh birthday, and they were going to visit Aunt Julia. Ivy ran up the steps of Aunt Julia's house and gave her aunt a big hug and kiss. Inside the house, in the middle of the living room, stood a box bigger than Ivy herself, wrapped in shiny silver paper and covered in blue and green ribbons. Aunt Julia said, "Happy birthday, Ivy!" Suddenly, the box started to move across the floor! What do *you* think happened next?

14

Long-john Pajamas

Do you have long-john pajamas? These warm and comfortable pajamas cover you from your neck to your ankles. Because long-john pajamas are all one piece of clothing, it is difficult to get out of them to go to the bathroom, so they have a handy "trapdoor" in the back!

Owl

Owls are large birds that stay awake at night. Animals that are active at night are called nocturnal. Keen eyesight and excellent hearing help owls find mice and other food in the dark. What do owls do during the daytime? They sleep! What sound does an owl make? *"Whoo, whoo!"*

15

Bobby Fischer

Bobby Fischer is considered the best chess player of all time. He got his first chess set when he was six years old and from that moment on he loved playing the game. At the age of twelve, Bobby was able to beat some of the greatest chess players in the country. He went on to win the U.S. junior championship at age fourteen, and as a young man, he won the world championship.

348

Pictures in the Sky

If you use your imagination when you look at the night sky, you'll see that some groups of stars form pictures, like a connect-the-dots puzzle. We call these groups of stars constellations. For centuries, different peoples told stories about the constellations, based on the shapes they saw when they connected the stars in the night sky. Many constellations were named after goddesses, gods, kings, queens, and heroes.

16

Pisces (Fish)

If your birthday is between February 19 and March 20, you are a Pisces. This sign is known for compassion and imagination. Its color is sea green. Its gemstone is the amethyst. Its animal is the fish. Pisces is represented by twin fish, mythical creatures that helped the Greek goddess Aphrodite defeat a huge sea monster.

347

Lightbulbs

*L*ightbulbs are everywhere! Think about what it would be like if there were no lightbulbs. There would be no reading in bed. You would have to brush your teeth by candlelight. Over a hundred years ago, most people did just that. But since Thomas Alva Edison invented the lightbulb in 1879, people all over the world can use electric light.

Chief Chef

Imagine you are a great chef. People come to your restaurant to try your delicious food. You are always busy in the kitchen, mixing dough, making soup, icing cookies, and building the tallest, tastiest sandwiches in the world. What are you going to cook up now?

346

Rain Gain

When clouds get heavy with water droplets, down comes the rain. Each raindrop gets bigger and bigger as it connects with other raindrops while it is falling. Rain is important to the Earth. It cleanses the air and gives many living things the water they need to live and grow.

18

Starstruck Scientists

Astronomers are scientists who study the night sky. These scientists are star experts. They study planets, constellations, moons, and meteors. They look through telescopes, watch comets and other objects move through space, and create star maps. If an astronomer discovers a new star or a comet in the sky, she can name it after herself!

345

Queen of the Night

The blossoms of most plants open up when the sun is bright in the sky. But some plants bloom at night. The queen of the night is a cactus whose reddish yellow flowers open after sunset. These cacti are originally from South America, but now many people keep them as house plants, too, because their flowers are so pretty.

Chicken

When you blink, wink, or close your eyes, your top eyelids move down to meet your bottom eyelids, like window shades for your eyes. When a chicken closes its eyes to go to sleep, its bottom eyelids, which are longer, move up to meet its top lids, closing the eyes from bottom to top.

344

Hey Diddle Diddle

Hey Diddle Diddle,
The cat and the fiddle,
The cow jumped over the moon.
The little dog laughed to see such sport,
And the dish ran away with the spoon.

20

Egyptian Pillows

When you go to sleep at night, do you like to lay your head down on your soft, fluffy pillow? People have been using pillows for centuries—but they weren't always soft! The people of ancient Egypt rested their heads on pillows made of wood or stone wrapped in cloth. Would you like a pillow made of stone?

343

Desert Sleepers

Can you imagine sleeping in the desert? The Tuareg, a tribe of people in Africa, do this every night. Tuareg families travel on camelback, herding goats, sheep, and cattle across the desert. When they find a good place to stop, they set up special tents made from woven grass, goat hair, blankets, and camel skins. The tents are good shelter against the cold of desert nights.

21

Rock-a-bye, Baby

Rock-a-bye, baby,
On the treetop,
When the wind blows,
The cradle will rock;
When the bough breaks,
The cradle will fall,
And down will come baby,
Cradle and all.

342

Sloth

The word *slothful* means slow and sluggish.
We get this word from the three-toed sloth—a real
slow-mover! The sloth, which lives in rain forests and
jungles, sleeps at least eighteen hours a day, hanging
from tree branches. The sloth is the slowest land
mammal. It eats fruits and berries—and anything else
that's slower than it is!

Mimosa

This plant is called *Mimosa pudica,* or "the sensitive plant." Its small, feathery leaves fold up when they are touched. If they are touched too hard, the leaves droop even more—but just a few minutes later, they lift themselves up again. And every night, the leaves close up until morning.

341

Shadows

What makes a shadow? Shadows are places unlit by the sun or other light sources. Since light can't shine through solid objects, they block the light, creating a shadow. Sometimes you can guess what an object is just by looking at the shape of its shadow. Have you ever played outside on a sunny day and watched your shadow move?

23

Weather Lore

The sun isn't always bright white—at sunrise and sunset, it can be golden or orange. Sometimes, low on the horizon, the sun glows a bright red. Many years ago, some people looked at the sun at dawn and dusk to predict the weather, saying, "Red sun at night, sailor's delight. Red sun at morning, sailor's warning." This meant that if the setting sun was red, the weather would be calm, safe for ships crossing the seas. But a red sun in the morning meant a storm was coming and sailors should be careful.

An Ant's-eye View

Close your eyes and imagine yourself very, very small. What if you got to be an ant for a day? What would the world look like? Blades of grass would be like tall trees—and people would look like giants! Ants are very social and live with lots of other ants in an anthill. Can you imagine how big your ant family would be?

Lamps

What did people use for light thousands of years ago, when they didn't have lightbulbs? Over fifty thousand years ago, people made the first stone lamps. Centuries later, the ancient Greeks and Romans made lamps of clay or bronze. They added a wick and burned oil made from nuts and olives.

Aries (Ram)

If your birthday is between March 21 and April 20, you are an Aries. This sign is known for strength, courage, and confidence. Its color is red. Its gemstone is the diamond. Its animal is the ram. In Greek mythology, Aries was the god of war—bold, aggressive, and courageous.

25

Hydra
(The Sea Serpent)

The biggest constellation in the sky is Hydra, the Sea Serpent. It looks like a long, winding snake. The Hydra was a powerful creature—only Hercules was able to slay it, after many battles.

338

Stevie Wonder

As a very young boy, Stevie Wonder sang in his church choir. By age nine, he had mastered the piano, drums, and harmonica. Though blind from birth, he never let this be a handicap and kept following his dream of becoming a performer. Stevie Wonder had his first hit song, called "Fingertips," when he was only twelve years old. People have been enjoying his music for over thirty years.

26

Platypus

The platypus is such an unusual animal that when scientists first saw one they thought someone had put it together as a joke! With a bill like a duck's, a tail like a beaver's, fur like an otter's, and webbed feet, the platypus is unlike any other animal. It goes out in the early evening and at dawn to look for food, using its snout to poke around at the bottom of lakes and streams. A flap of skin covers its ears and eyes, protecting them as it swims.

Nightcap

Snuggling under a blanket keeps you warm, but what about your head? A nightcap does the trick! Nightcaps were much more common many years ago, before people had heating systems built into their homes. But some people still wear them on very cold nights.

Stepping into TV

Marc flipped through the TV channels. "Boring," he sighed. Suddenly, he came to a cartoon show. The characters were joking and playing together, then one of them turned and shouted, "Hey, Marc, come on in!" Marc was stunned. All the cartoon characters waved and cheered. He stood up, put one foot into the TV, then the other, and stepped all the way into the cartoon. What do *you* think happened next?

Moon Phases

Every month, the moon seems to go through changes of shape and size. These changes are called the phases of the moon. The moon's shape isn't really different; it just looks that way because different parts of it are in Earth's shadow. When the moon is big, bright, and round, it's a full moon. When it's completely in Earth's shadow and can hardly be seen, it's called a new moon.

28

Snore Roar

Some people don't make any noise when they sleep. But other people snore very loudly! Sometimes a person snores because he has a cold or allergies and his lungs need to work harder to bring in air. The extra effort causes a noisy vibration in his mouth and throat. Snoring doesn't hurt you, but it might keep other people in your family awake!

335

Bus Driver

Have you ever ridden on a bus? Whether it's a big yellow school bus or a city bus, there is a bus driver at the wheel. Some cities have buses that pick up and deliver passengers all night long. Driving a bus takes lots of practice. The driver has to know how to move the bus in and out of tight corners, how to drive safely in snow and rain, and which back roads to take when a main road is closed.

29

Top

Tops have been spinning for a long time. The earliest tops were made of clay. Their inventors carved pictures of people and animals on them. Toy makers in ancient Japan were the first to put holes in them. This made the air whistle as it rushed through the holes of the spinning top.

Shaving in Space

Gravity makes things fall to the ground and keeps everything from floating away. But in space, there is no gravity. When the astronauts first went up in space, they had a few unexpected problems! When they shaved, for example, their whiskers flew all around the inside of the spaceship because there was no gravity to make them fall! Scientists had to create a special kind of razor with a little vacuum cleaner attached to it that sucks up the whiskers.

30

I'm Ready Now

Yes, I am, I'm ready now,
I think I can go to sleep.
Oh, wait, there's something I forgot.
Oh, never mind, there's really not.
Yes, I am, I'm ready now.
See? I've closed my eyes.
But wait, oh please don't go away.
I forgot to...what did I just say?
Yes, I am, I'm ready now,
I'm almost fast asleep.
But, wait, can you turn on that light?
Oh, never mind.
Good night.

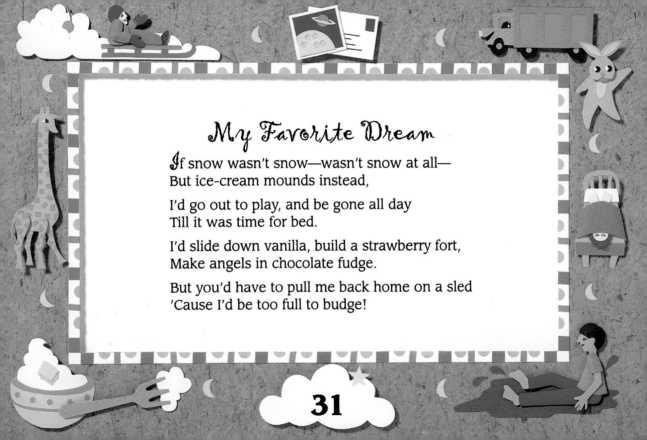

My Favorite Dream

If snow wasn't snow—wasn't snow at all—
But ice-cream mounds instead,

I'd go out to play, and be gone all day
Till it was time for bed.

I'd slide down vanilla, build a strawberry fort,
Make angels in chocolate fudge.

But you'd have to pull me back home on a sled
'Cause I'd be too full to budge!

Navigation

A long time ago, before there was modern equipment, sailors navigated, or guided their travels, across the oceans by using the movements of the sun, moon, and stars. The sun rises in the east and sets in the west; shadows point in the same direction, north or south, depending on which hemisphere you live in; and of course the North Star always points north. Sailors also used maps and charts, which showed where to look for certain constellations in the sky.

Hula Hoop

Children have played with hoops for about three thousand years. In ancient Egypt, Greece, and Rome, hoops were made from dried grapevines. Hula hoops became very popular in the United States in 1958. During one six-month period, adults and children twirled and spun twenty million hula hoops! Hula hoop contests and marathons—where whoever spins his or her hoop around the body longest wins—were common events.

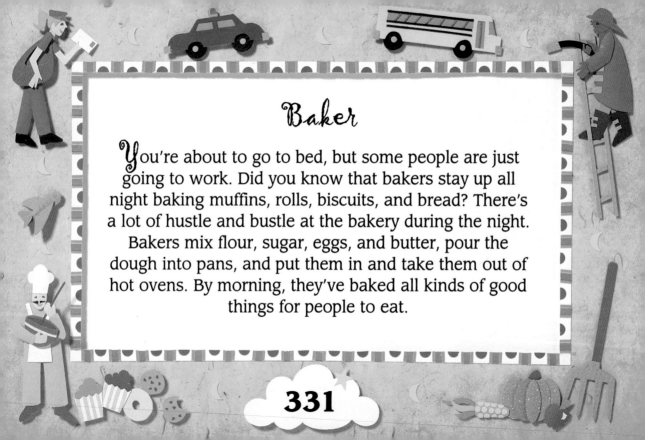

Baker

You're about to go to bed, but some people are just going to work. Did you know that bakers stay up all night baking muffins, rolls, biscuits, and bread? There's a lot of hustle and bustle at the bakery during the night. Bakers mix flour, sugar, eggs, and butter, pour the dough into pans, and put them in and take them out of hot ovens. By morning, they've baked all kinds of good things for people to eat.

331

Ticktock, Body Clock

Everyone has a body clock. It's a kind of constant rhythm that tells you when it's time to eat, sleep, and wake up. Daylight, darkness, and temperature seem to play a part in keeping the clock regular. Do you notice that you get hungry or sleepy at the same time every day? That's your body clock at work.

33

First Men on the Moon

The very first time a person landed on the moon was July 20, 1969. The United States sent three brave men—Neil Armstrong, Edwin "Buzz" Aldrin, and Michael Collins—up to explore the moon's surface. Mr. Armstrong and Mr. Aldrin walked around on the moon for about two and a half hours, while Mr. Collins orbited the moon twenty-five times. Then the moon lander hooked up with the orbiting capsule, and the first men on the moon went back to Earth.

330

The Shooting Star

Matthew lay in bed trying to go to sleep. He decided to count the stars shining through his bedroom window. "One, two, three," he counted, "four, five—" Suddenly, the fifth star got brighter and brighter, then streaked across the sky. A moment later, it came right in through Matthew's window. Glowing with warmth, the star floated next to the bed. A note attached to it read, "For Matthew." What do *you* think happened next?

Cot

One very simple type of bed is a cot. Cots are very handy because they can be opened up quickly and easily, then folded up again and stored in the closet. Cots are useful on camping trips and also as extra beds for company.

Tarsier

$\mathcal{T}$he tiny tarsier (pronounced TAR-see-ur) is about the size of a kitten, but its eyes are enormous. These animals live in the rain forests of Asia. Looking for food at night is easy for them because their eyesight is so sharp. Tarsiers can also turn their heads almost all the way around to the back! What would it be like if you could do that?

35

Steffi Graf

Steffi Graf did something no tennis player had ever done before. When she was only nineteen years old, she won four Grand Slam tournaments and the Olympic Gold Medal. It all began when Steffi was four years old and begged her father to give her tennis lessons. He finally took an old racket and sawed the handle down so it was just her size. Two years later, she went on to win her first tournament!

Orion
(The Hunter)

In ancient Greek tales, Orion was a skillful, brave hunter. To find Orion, look for three stars in a row in the winter sky. These stars form Orion's belt. The best time to see Orion is December through March.

Aquarius (Water Bearer)

If your birthday is between January 21 and February 18, you are an Aquarius. This sign is known for originality, creativity, and independence. Its color is electric blue. Its gemstone is the sapphire. Its animal is the bird. In the zodiac, Aquarius is the water bearer, a prince who once filled the drinking cups of the gods and goddesses living on Mount Olympus.

Firefly Flickers

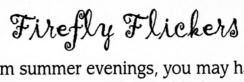

On warm summer evenings, you may have seen little flickers of greenish light blinking in fields, gardens, and lawns. These are fireflies! The firefly's light is made by chemicals in its stomach, or abdomen. It blinks on and off to send messages to other fireflies. These insects are sometimes called lightning bugs.

Interesting Inventions

*I*magine what it would be like to be an inventor. What would you invent? A new toy? A better bicycle? What tools and materials would you use to make your inventions?

Animal Weather-Forecasters

Animals act differently in different weather conditions. Before a rainstorm, insects crawl deeper into the grass, and swallows, trying to catch them, fly lower in the sky. Some people watch how animals behave and try to predict the weather based on what they see. Have you ever noticed your pet or another animal acting strangely when the weather is about to change?

Smoke Detector

A smoke detector protects people when they sleep at night. If there's any smoke in the air, the smoke detector sounds an alarm. It buzzes or beeps loudly, over and over. The loud sound awakens the sleepers so they can take care of the fire. What should you do if you hear the smoke alarm during the night? Get out fast.

Venus's-flytrap

Did you know that some plants actually eat insects? One type of insect-eating plant is the Venus's-flytrap. It has special feelers on its leaves that tell it when a fly has landed. When the fly gets stuck on the sticky leaves, the leaves snap shut around it like a clam's shell. The soil these plants live in doesn't give them enough food, so they eat insects to get extra nourishment.

Bear

The bear spends the summer and fall eating lots of food and building up its stores of body fat. When winter comes, it curls up in a safe place, such as a cave, and sleeps very deeply. Its breathing and heart rate slow down. Occasionally, the bear will wake up in milder winter weather, poke its head out, and wander around looking for food.

Baa, Baa, Black Sheep

Baa, baa, black sheep,
Have you any wool?
Yes, sir; yes, sir;
Three bags full.
One for my master,
And one for my dame,
And one for the little boy
Who lives down the lane.

40

Siesta Time

Do you remember a day that was so hot that you felt sleepy? In some countries, people stop to take a rest during the hottest part of the day. In Mexico, they call this rest time a siesta. Everyone stops working and takes a break. Later in the afternoon, people go back to work.

Hammock Hangout

Native American tribes living in the Amazon rain forests sleep in hammocks. A hammock is a special net, usually tied between two trees, that can hold a person above the ground and swing them comfortably to sleep. The rain forest stays warm all night, so the native peoples don't even need blankets.

41

Stars

I'm glad the stars are over me
And not beneath my feet,
Where we should trample on them
Like cobbles on the street.
I think it is a happy thing
That they are set so far;
It's best to have to look up high
When you would see a star.

Gorilla

Young gorillas and birds have something in common—both make a nice cozy nest from branches, leaves, and twigs. Young gorillas and mother gorillas with babies put together quick, simple nests in the trees for daytime naps. In the evening, they build sturdier nests for nightlong sleep.

Legumes

Have you ever eaten a legume? Legumes are plants whose seeds grow inside a pod. Peas, string beans, and peanuts are legumes—and they're tasty and nutritious, too! Legumes bend their leaves toward the sun during the day, but when it gets dark, the leaves fold up.

321

Glowworms

Glowworms are young fireflies, or firefly larvae. They live in dark, moist places, inside rotting logs and among leaves. When the weather gets hot and rain is on the way, they come out and look for food. It takes two years from the time they hatch for glowworms to grow into fireflies.

43

Water Fall

Water falls to the ground in many forms: hail, rain, sleet, snow, and more. Water that falls from clouds to the ground is called precipitation. If you collected all the Earth's precipitation for a year, do you know how much water you would have? Enough water for every person in the United States to take nine hundred baths a day!

320

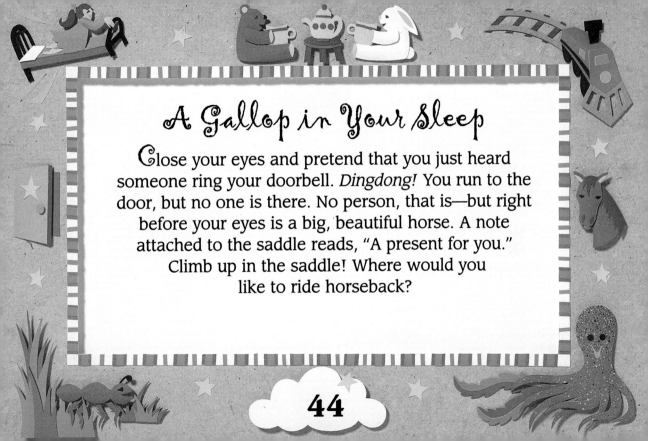

A Gallop in Your Sleep

Close your eyes and pretend that you just heard someone ring your doorbell. *Dingdong!* You run to the door, but no one is there. No person, that is—but right before your eyes is a big, beautiful horse. A note attached to the saddle reads, "A present for you." Climb up in the saddle! Where would you like to ride horseback?

Candle Clock

Where have you seen candles being used? Maybe on birthday cakes, dinner tables, or for holiday celebrations? In the Middle Ages, people used candles to tell time. They marked lines down the side of a large candle, one line for each hour. As time passed, the candle burned down, showing how many hours had gone by. Candles are made of wax, sometimes decorated with bright colors. The candle flame burns on a wick, a piece of thick string inside the wax.

Elvis Presley

Elvis Presley was born into a very poor family. He grew up without brothers or sisters and always felt as if he didn't quite fit in with other kids. One thing that made him very happy, though, was singing in his church choir every Sunday. When he was only ten, his singing won second prize in a talent contest. A year later, his parents gave him his first guitar. He went on to become one of the most popular rock 'n' roll singers of all time.

Sirius
(The Dog Star)

Sirius, often called the Dog Star, is the brightest star in the night sky and one of our closest star neighbors. It's part of the constellation Canis Major, the Great Dog. Another constellation not far from the Great Dog is Canis Minor, the Little Dog.

The Dog Star

Tent

It's fun to sleep in a tent! Tents can be quickly put together or taken apart, and can be made of many different materials such as grass or goat hair. Some desert people sleep in tents every night. Have you ever slept in a tent on a camping trip? You may have slept in a tent made of cloth or plastic.

Bush Baby

Bush babies are small, furry, nocturnal animals named for their shrill, piercing calls that sound like the shouts of excited children. These creatures sleep all day long. At night, they look for food—insects, small lizards, and fruit. Their big, bulging eyes can see very well in the dark. They can catch a mosquito in midair! And their huge ears pick up every small sound—they can hear even the tiniest insects. At dawn, they go back to sleep with their ears folded shut.

Moonprints

When the astronauts walked on the moon, they made huge footprints with their moon boots. Because the moon has no wind, water, or weather, the footprints will stay unchanged on the surface of the moon forever—unless, of course, they are disturbed by other moon visitors.

Sleeping on Ceilings

Bess was going to her first sleepover at Jill's house. She packed her pajamas, her toothbrush, and clean clothes for the next day. She walked up to Jill's front door and knocked. "Come in!" Jill called. But when Bess stepped through the doorway, she found herself walking on the ceiling! Every room in Jill's house was upside down. What do *you* think happened next?

Carpenter

Carpenters are builders. They drill holes, hammer nails, and saw wood. Carpenters who build and repair the backgrounds, or stage sets, in theaters often work at night. They start their work after the play is over. When the actors and audience come to the theater for the next performance, the stage, often with brand-new sets, is ready for the show!

48

Catching a Yawn

When you tell a joke or tickle someone, you can make them laugh. Did you know that by yawning, you can make someone else yawn? When you yawn, you open your mouth wide and take a deep breath, bringing a rush of air into your lungs. Scientists still don't know why yawns are catching. What do you think?

315

Mars

Many different kinds of spacecraft have been sent to Mars to study it. But could anybody actually live there? It has a very pleasant high temperature of around 60 degrees—about as warm as a day in early spring. But people couldn't ever survive the low temperature—*minus* 220 degrees! That's colder than any place on Earth, even the South Pole!

Crossword Puzzle

Words down, words across. That's what crossword puzzles are made of. A man named Arthur Lynne invented this game, which consists of a grid that is filled in with words. Readers are given clues to try and figure out the correct word. Crossword puzzles are very popular—some are simple, while others have dozens of words and take hours to complete.

Mud

Ooo-ooo whee! It feels so good to me.
I love to squish it in my hands,
It's gushy, mushy, mud.
Ooo-ooo whee! I can make my own for free.
Just take some dirt and wet it till
It's gushy, mushy, mud.
And when you see this mud and dirt
All over my good pants and shirt,
At least you'll know no one got hurt.
And when you have to clean this place
Of all this mud—what a disgrace—
At least there won't be quite as much
As I've got on my face!

A Very Special Tent

What if you were sleeping
In a very special tent,
With a peephole just for looking out
And a tiny little vent?

Nobody would bother you.
You'd have lots of food to eat,
Snacks and games and books to read.
Wouldn't that be neat?

Maybe you would stay awake
Counting all the stars.
Maybe you'd be visited
By friendly guys from Mars.

It would be such fun to sleep
In a very special tent,
With a peephole just for looking out
And a tiny little vent.

Frisbee

The Frisbie Pie Company in Connecticut made their homemade pies in pans labeled with the company's name. College students invented a game of tossing pie pans to each other—since they were flat, the pans easily flew through the air. This game was nicknamed Frisbie-ing. Walter Frederick Morrison saw the students playing with pie pans, and made a plastic flying disk shaped like a pie pan, which he called the Frisbee.

51

Polaris

Since people have learned to guide their journeys by the stars, Polaris has been the most reliable marker in the sky. Also called the polestar or the North Star, Polaris is directly over the North Pole. So when you find Polaris, you also find the direction north. And unlike the other stars in the sky, Polaris does not move, so you can always travel by it.

Sleep Talking

Some people talk in their sleep! No one really knows why this happens. Sleep talking usually occurs during very deep sleep, and it isn't unusual. Though it's sometimes impossible to make any sense of what sleep talkers are saying, they are usually talking about things that happened during the day.

Farmer

Early in the morning, the farm is dark and quiet. But the farmers are already up and working. They milk the cows, shear the sheep for their wool, and collect chicken eggs. They plow the fields of wheat, oats, and corn. Farmers work very hard taking care of their farms, which give us many things we eat and use every day.

The Rocket

Sarah and Joseph, ten-year-old twins, are the youngest people ever to go up in a rocket into space. They climb into the capsule, strap themselves in, and turn on their communication radios. Mission control orders the countdown over the radio: "Here we go. Ten, nine, eight, seven, six, five, four, three, two, one—ignition—blastoff!" Sarah and Joseph look out the rocket window and see the Earth grow farther and farther away. In just a few hours they'll be in outer space and ready to begin their assignment. What do *you* think happens next?

53

Moon Gate

In ancient China, families celebrated nighttime by going out to the garden and watching the full moon rise. They did this especially in October to celebrate the fall Moon Festival. At other times they went out to enjoy the spicy fragrance of the night-blooming moon flower. They even built circle-shaped gates in the garden, called Moon Gates.

Kit Fox

*O*ut in the dark desert night, the kit fox looks for food.
This animal is the size of a small dog. Its very large
ears give it excellent hearing—it can hear almost
everything, even tiny bugs scurrying under the sand!
Bugs are one of its favorite foods, and all it has to do to
find them is listen. If you listen very carefully now,
what sounds can *you* hear?

54

Murphy Bed

If you lived in a small apartment that didn't have room for much furniture, where would you put your bed? Maybe you'd have a Murphy bed—a bed actually hidden inside the wall. You could just reach up and pull down a handle from the wall, and the bed would fold out. In the morning, you could fold the bed back up into the wall, and no one would even know it's there.

The King

Cepheus is the name of the king in the night sky. Search the sky for a constellation that looks like a drawing of a house, with lots of stars inside it. The best time to see Cepheus is in late fall and early winter.

Judy Garland

Judy Garland was the young actress who played Dorothy in the movie *The Wizard of Oz.* Her real name was Frances Ethel Gumm. Her older sisters were performers, too. When she was only two and a half years old, brave little Frances ran up on stage with them to sing. A big movie studio hired her at age thirteen and she went on to become one of the most beloved stars of all time.

308

Streetlights

Streetlights help people see their way along
public streets in the dark. They also make streets safer
late at night. The first streetlights were candle lanterns
outside people's homes. Later, the streets were lit by
the burning of oil lamps. Today, our streetlights use
electricity. What do you think it would be like to have
to change one of the lightbulbs on a streetlight?

Capricorn (Goat)

If your birthday is between December 22 and January 20, you are a Capricorn. This sign is known for being ambitious, funny, and practical. Its color is dark gray. Its gemstone is jet. Its animal is the goat. In the zodiac, Capricorn is a creature with the head and body of a goat and the tail of a fish.

307

Snow Days

The next time you catch snowflakes on your mitten, take a closer look. You will see that every snowflake has six sides, but no two are exactly alike. Each has a unique pattern unlike any other snowflake. Snow falls in winter or on high mountaintops, where it's always cold. But snow, piled deep, can also act as a blanket, keeping things warm.

Town Underground

Imagine that you're lying on the beach. Everyone around you is tanning in the sun, but you decide to dig a tunnel in the sand. You dig deeper and deeper until you're far underground. Suddenly, you look up. You've dug a tunnel to another city! What happens next?

Night Attraction

The bright, beautiful colors of some flowers attract bees, insects, and birds during the day. Other plants have adapted to attract moths and bats at night. These plants have night-blooming flowers that are usually white or very light-colored. This makes them easier to see in the dark.

Counting Sheep

If you have trouble falling asleep, try counting sheep. It's easy to do. Just close your eyes and imagine sheep jumping over a fence, one by one. Many people find that this calming, repeated picture makes them feel drowsy, and they drift off to sleep. How many sheep can you count before you fall asleep?

305

Little Jack Horner

Little Jack Horner
Sat in the corner,
Eating a Christmas pie.
He stuck in his thumb,
And pulled out a plum,
And said, "What a good boy am I!"

Python

The python is the largest snake in all of Africa—it can grow to be over thirty feet long. The python looks for food at night and spends the day coiled up on tree branches, resting during the hot afternoon. Sometimes a python will eat a huge meal and be so full that it can sleep for six months without eating again—it will take that long to digest its food.

Dark All Day

What do you think it would be like if it were dark outside in the middle of the day? People who live in Hammerfest, a town in Norway, know what it's like. From November to the end of January, it's dark all night and all day. But when the month of May comes, just the opposite happens: the sun shines all day and all through the night until the end of July.

Painting Stories

The Aborigine people of Australia paint pictures while they tell stories to their children. The paintings are called "Dreamtime" pictures—they show the different characters and scenes from the story. The children memorize the stories and learn to paint these pictures on their own, so they can share them with their own children some day.

303

Parrot Fish

Can you imagine napping in a bubble? The parrot fish, which lives in warm oceans, does just that. As it's getting ready to take a rest, it produces a jellylike liquid that it wraps around itself. This coating protects the parrot fish while it rests. Later, it breaks out of the bubble and swims away.

Purple Cow

I never saw a purple cow,
I never hope to see one.
But I can tell you anyhow,
I'd rather see than be one.

Arctic

*L*ong ago, the ancient Greeks saw a group of stars in the northern sky that looked like the shape of a bear. They named it the Great Bear. Much later, explorers in the far north named the land by the North Pole after this constellation. The name of the land is the Arctic, which comes from the Greek word *arktos*, meaning "bear."

Wild Ginger

Wild ginger is a North American plant that grows wild and thrives in shady places. It doesn't attract bees, but is pollinated and its nectar gathered by a beetle that climbs right into the middle of it. Early settlers collected the roots and ground them up to use as a spice, and also as a cure for stomachaches.

Invisible You

*I*magine that you are invisible. Just think of all the places you could go—and no one would know you were there! You could watch wild animals in the forest, and they wouldn't run away because they couldn't see you! You could help a friend run a magic show, holding objects in the air so it would look as if they're floating. What would you do if you were invisible?

Wind Sock

The wind doesn't wear socks, but there is such a thing as a wind sock. A wind sock is a wide, soft tube of cloth or plastic that looks like a bright-colored sock on a stick. When the wind blows, it fills the sock with air. The sock shows the direction of the wind blowing through it. Airline pilots rely on the wind sock to find out the wind's direction—their planes must take off facing the wind, and the wind sock shows them which way to go.

300

Taurus (Bull)

If your birthday is between April 21 and May 21, you are a Taurus. This sign is known for determination, patience, and warmheartedness. Its color is green. Its gemstone is emerald. Its animal is the bull. Taurus is named after the Minotaur, a creature from Greek mythology that had the head of a bull and the body of a man.

Laser Power

Laser light is a kind of artificial light that's very bright and strong. A laser is so strong that it can cut through steel and concrete, yet its narrow beam is delicate enough to perform surgery and make compact discs. Laser light can shine a long, long way without fading— scientists have used it to measure the distance between the Earth and the moon.

299

Shirley Temple

When Shirley Temple was only three years old, an agent came to see if she wanted to be in a movie—and she hid under her dance teacher's piano. But by the time she was five, she was singing and dancing her way to movie stardom. Only two years later, Shirley was the first child actor to receive an Academy Award.

65

The Telescope

The stars and planets are far, far away—which is why they look so small. But how do scientists know so much about the stars and planets when they're so far out in space? One way is by looking through giant telescopes. They make things millions of miles away look bigger and clearer. The first telescope was invented by a spectacle maker, Hans Lipperhey, almost four hundred years ago.

Tooth Fairy

When one of your baby teeth falls out, leave it under your pillow when you go to bed that night. The tooth fairy will come and take it, leaving you a small gift or money in its place. This fairy legend is popular in the United States. In other countries, the story is about a mouse who collects baby teeth.

Whippoorwill

*I*f you listen carefully when darkness comes, maybe you can hear the sound of the whippoorwills. These birds call out to one another, *"Whippoorwill, whippoorwill!"* Their cry means, "Don't come too close, this territory is mine!" Sometimes each bird will call 100 times in a row. Whippoorwills swoop close to the ground to catch and eat all kinds of insects.

Rip Van Winkle

One American myth is the story of a man named Rip Van Winkle. He and his faithful dog, Wolf, hiked deep into the woods one day. He met a group of dwarfs there and joined them in games and merriment. The dwarfs offered him a special drink that made him sleep for twenty years. After he woke up, he found out that he had slept through the entire Revolutionary War and had grown a long, long beard.

Swimming Surprise

Emily and her family had just moved into their new house. But this was no ordinary house—this house was underwater! Every night they put on their diving suits and went out to explore the sea. Tonight, an extra special surprise was in store. An amazing creature was waiting for them, swimming around the side of the house. What do *you* think happened next?

Igloo

In the cold, northernmost part of North America, a Native American tribe, the Inuit, once lived in homes made of bricks. But these were no ordinary bricks—they were made of ice and packed snow. These ice-brick homes were called igloos. Though snow and ice are very cold, these thick, tightly packed bricks actually kept out the cold. The people inside the igloos stayed warm.

Good-Night Stretch

Stretching is a good way to relax before you go to bed. Lie as flat as you can on your back with your legs straight, and reach your arms back and up above your head. Now stretch your whole body, from the tips of your fingers to the tips of your toes. Hold that stretch, count to three, and relax.

295

The Man in the Moon

Who is the man in the moon? Sometimes the full moon looks like a big round face smiling down at the Earth. The moon's surface has many holes, craters, and bumps that from far away look like eyes, a nose, and a mouth! Next time there is a full moon, see if you can find the man in the moon.

Board Games

There are thousands of board games played all over the world. But who thought of the first one? In 1920, archaeologists discovered a game board at the site of an ancient city. They found dice and other playing pieces. This is believed to be one of the first board games ever played—it's almost five thousand years old.

Telephone Operator

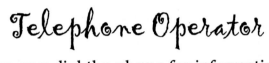

When you dial the phone for information, an operator is there to answer. Telephone operators give out telephone numbers, help people make long-distance calls, and put calls through in an emergency. Some operators work all through the night. That way someone is always at the other end of the phone, ready to help.

70

My Slippers

I have a pair of slippers
I'll never throw away.
They're dirty, torn, and full of stains,
But I wear them every day.

They fit my feet like mittens,
They're blue and green and red.
And Mommy doesn't know this,
But I wear them in my bed.

They help me get to places
I travel to in my dreams,
Even though my toes stick through
The torn and ripped-up seams.

293

Meteors

Every night shooting stars flash across the sky. Shooting stars, or meteors, are not really stars, but chunks of rock or metal burning up as they pass through our planet's atmosphere. Meteors fall into Earth's atmosphere during the day, too, but the sky is then too bright for us to see them. When many meteors fall at one time, it's called a meteor shower.

Pluto

Pluto was the last planet in our solar system to be discovered. It's also the smallest planet, even smaller than our moon. Because it's so far from the sun, the average temperature on Pluto is supercold: minus 364 degrees! Its year is very long, too—it takes 248 Earth years for Pluto to orbit the sun once.

Topsy-turvy Sleep

When I am snuggled in at night
And ready to fall asleep,
I tuck my hands right under my face,
I put my bear in his special place,
And I don't make a peep.

So how come in the morning
When I wake, I'm upside down?
My feet are where my head should be,
My bear is on the ground.

One pillow's underneath my feet,
The other's twisted in the sheet.
My blankets lie there in a heap,
My toes are buried layers deep.
You'd think I went off dancing
Instead of off to sleep!

Zookeeper

It's 9:00 A.M., and the animals are hungry! Who feeds them? The zookeeper. Zookeepers are trained to know all about the animals at the zoo. They make sure they are well-fed and healthy, and that their homes are safe and clean. Zookeepers know how to help if an animal is sick, upset, or going to have a baby. Some zoos have special chow for each kind of animal—they feed zebra chow to the zebras and elephant chow to the elephants!

291

Kite

Kites were first used in China in 1200 B.C. Decorated with special colors and patterns, they were used to send messages and signals. In 1752, American scientist and inventor Benjamin Franklin used a kite to learn more about lightning and electricity. Kites have also been useful tools in predicting the weather. Today, people fly kites just for fun or in kite-flying competitions. They buy and make kites in many different shapes and colors.

73

Pig Moon

People all over the world believe that events in nature are influenced by the phases of the moon. East Indians have special names for times when the moon appears more than half full but less than full: "little pig moon" and "big pig moon." During these two moon phases, their pigs always seem to get overly excited, breaking free from their pens to wander off into the fields.

A Long Night's Sleep

How long do you sleep? Some people need a lot of sleep, while others feel rested after only a short nap. Little babies need *lots* of rest—they can sleep as much as sixteen to twenty hours a day. Children need about ten hours of sleep and most grown-ups need about seven or eight hours. How much sleep you need can also depend on how busy you were during the day.

Water Bed

$\mathcal{A}$ water bed is a bed you can float on! When you lie down on a water bed, the mattress, which is filled with water, gently rocks you back and forth. It's a very relaxing and comfortable place to sleep. Water beds have been around for a long time. Thousands of years ago, the ancient Egyptians built water beds and Queen Cleopatra slept on one.

289

Magic Marshmallow

On a cold winter's day, David ran inside and sat down to have a cup of delicious hot chocolate. In front of him was a bag of large, squishy marshmallows. He plopped two into his cup. Then, to David's surprise, the other marshmallows began to move and wiggle their way out of the bag. One by one, they jumped onto the floor and bounced, single file, right out the kitchen door! David had to follow them. What do *you* think happened next?

75

Jesse Owens

Jesse Owens was one of the most incredible Olympic athletes who ever lived. He was born in Alabama and moved to Ohio when he was seven. In junior high school, he tried out for the track team and ran the 100-yard dash in only ten seconds! While in college, he broke records in running and long jumping. Later, Jesse won four gold medals at the Olympic games in Germany in 1936, and set seven world records in his entire career.

288

Leopard

The leopard prowls through the thick brush of the African forest. This large cat is a very good climber and often carries its prey into the branches of a tree to keep it safe from other hungry animals. It hunts for food at night, using its sensitive whiskers to help guide it in the dark. The leopard's black spots make it difficult to see in the forest so that it can sneak up on its prey without being noticed.

Diver's Discovery

Imagine that you have just dived into the ocean. As you swim deeper and deeper, you see a strange shape sticking up out of the sandy bottom. You take a closer look—it's a half-buried treasure chest! A sign on it says, "Open me." You slowly open the lid. What's inside?

The Northern Crown

Forming the shape of a beautiful crown, this constellation is well-known by many cultures. The bright star in the center is Gemma, the crown jewel. Look for the crown in the night sky from April through August.

Under an Umbra

You've probably seen an umbra, but you just didn't know it. *Umbra* is the Latin word for shadow. In fact, umbra is part of a word you do know—*umbrella*. An umbrella can keep you dry in the rain, or provide shade on a sunny day.

Flashlight Fish

It's very dark in the deepest parts of the ocean. But one type of fish has no problem with that—it carries its own flashlight everywhere it goes. Under each eye, the flashlight fish has a tiny pouch that glows. These little "flashlights" help the fish to see in the dark. If the flashlight fish doesn't want to be seen, it turns off its lights by closing the little pouches.

Shark

Sharks swim swiftly and silently in the ocean. Most sharks are good hunters and fast swimmers, but there's a catch: They must always keep moving forward—even when they're resting—or they'll sink! Like fish, most kinds of sharks don't actually sleep— but they do slow down to rest.

All about Autumn

Autumn is a time for change. Animals store food and get their homes ready for winter. Tree leaves change colors and fall to the ground. Nighttime creeps in earlier and lasts longer. The air becomes crisp and cool, and frost appears on the ground. In autumn, farmers harvest crops: apples, wheat, corn, and other foods. What do you like best about autumn?

Coyote and the Stars

According to a Native American tale, one night the gods told Coyote to take all the stars and put them in special places in the sky. Coyote took the stars and set off on his task. But he was so sleepy that he tripped and fell. The stars scattered in all directions, creating the bright patterns we see them in now.

284

Evening Primrose

The late afternoon gently arrives, and the sun is no longer high in the sky. Although you might be getting a bit tired, this is a favorite time for the evening primrose. These yellow flowers begin to open at the end of the day and blossom all night long. When the night is over and a new day begins, their petals close up tight again.

80

Itsy-bitsy Spider

The itsy-bitsy spider
Climbed up the waterspout;
Down came the rain
And washed the spider out;
Out came the sun
And dried up all the rain;
And the itsy-bitsy spider
Climbed up the spout again.

Three Blind Mice

Three blind mice,
See how they run!
They all ran after the farmer's wife,
Who cut off their tails with a carving knife.
Did you ever see such a sight in your life,
As three blind mice?

81

Light and Color

What brings out the color in many flowering plants? Sunlight! In an experiment, scientists took some young plants and put them in a dark room without any light. After some time, the colors changed: the stems that should have been green were yellow, and the flowers had no color. When the plants were put back in the sunlight, their natural colors returned after only three hours.

282

Shadow Play

*S*hadow plays are puppet shows where you don't see the puppets! Behind a large screen, the puppeteer holds puppets and makes them move. Light shining onto the screen from behind casts shadows, and the audience sees the puppets' shadows move and act out stories. In Indonesia, shadow plays are called *wayang kulit.* They tell stories of heroes, monsters, kings, gods, and goddesses from Hindu myths. The shows last all night long.

82

Stormy Blessing

What is a monsoon? It's a wind that blows across tropical areas in different parts of the world. In many countries, the monsoons blow for almost six months straight, bringing moisture from the oceans in the form of dark clouds and rain. Six months sounds like a long time for it to rain, but many farmers are happy when the monsoons come because the wet weather is good for their crops. After six months, the winds change direction and the rain stops—until the next monsoon season.

281

Sea Otter

Sea otters spend almost their entire lives in the water. Before they go to sleep, they wrap themselves in a blanket of kelp, a kind of seaweed. Kelp grows in enormous bunches, called beds, that are firmly attached to the ocean floor or to rocks far below the surface of the waves. Like an anchor, the kelp keeps the snoozing otters from floating away.

Neon Bright

eon lights are thin tubes of colored glass bent in the shapes of letters or pictures. Gases in the tube are combined with energy in a way that makes the gases glow and create light. Neon lights make bright, colorful signs and advertisements. Also, because neon lights can shine clearly through fog, they are used at airports around the world.

Snail

Snails can be seen day or night. They often gather in warm, damp places. You might find them up in a tree, in a garden, or even on a wall. The part that looks like the snail's belly is really its foot. The snail's scientific name is *gastropod*, which means "belly foot."

Hercules

Hercules was one of the first constellations to be named, honoring the strong and brave hero of many legends.
He fought many monsters, including a scorpion, a lion, and a crab. If you look carefully, you can see him in the night sky from May through October.

279

Bed Flight

Imagine yourself in your bed, safely tucked in on all sides. Suddenly the bed begins to shake and quiver, and finally lets loose and zooms through the window into the sky! There you are in your bed floating happily among the clouds. Your pillow helps you steer, and your stuffed animals are your fellow passengers. Where would you like to go?

85

Moth

If you turn on an outdoor light at night, what are the first creatures to come and visit? Probably the moths! Moths are flying insects that are active at night. They navigate by keeping their eyes on the moon. Twisting and turning, they try to fly on a steady path along the moon's rays. They are attracted to burning lightbulbs in the same way, gathering at streetlights, porch lights, and lanterns.

Gemini (Twins)

If your birthday is between May 22 and June 21, you are a Gemini. This sign is known for wit, energy, and talkativeness. Its color is yellow. Its gemstone is topaz. Its animal is the monkey. Gemini is named after a set of twin brothers in Greek mythology—one was immortal, and the other was not.

Supersneakers

One quiet evening, Jules decided to clean out his closet. He found toys, games, and books that he had forgotten about. Way in the back of the closet, he found a pair of old, worn-out sneakers, and he put them on. Right before his eyes, his feet started to grow! They grew and grew until his feet were as long as the room. What do *you* think happened next?

277

Sally Ride

Sally Ride was the first American woman in space, blasting off in the *Challenger* space shuttle in 1983. As a young child, Sally was mainly interested in sports. She played ball with the boys in her neighborhood, and practiced to become a tennis champion. Whenever she saw astronauts on TV, Sally never imagined that space travel would be possible for women. In spite of this, as a young woman, she applied to NASA's space program and was chosen over eight thousand other people.

87

Voice Box Vibrations

Place your fingers gently on your throat and say, "ahhhh." Can you feel your voice box moving? The voice box is like a musical instrument in your throat that produces sounds. Sometimes you can see your voice box vibrate in the mirror. You can even change the volume of your instrument, just like you can pluck a guitar string harder to make a louder sound.

276

Dream Catcher

A dream catcher is a wooden hoop with deerskin woven around and through it in a pattern like a spider's web, with a small round hole in the middle. It is decorated with beads, jewels, and feathers and is hung over children's beds. Native American lore says that good dreams flow through the center hole while bad dreams get caught and tangled in the web. The sun's rays shine through in the morning and destroy the bad dreams.

Roller Skates

The first roller skates were made by a man named Joseph Merlin, who built musical instruments for a living. He made the skates to wear at a costume party, so he could roll from room to room while playing his violin. But Mr. Merlin forgot one thing: the rubber stoppers! He crashed into a mirror, breaking both the mirror and his violin. Roller skates have been improved a lot since then!

Moon Future

Scientists hope to send more people to the moon in future space programs. They have even thought about creating a colony on the moon, where people from Earth can live for some time. They also think the moon could be used as a rest stop on the way to other planets.

89

Bedtime Ritual

I think I'll take my own sweet time
To relax and clear this head of mine.

I'm going to stretch my arms and toes,
Take a deep breath in, then blow my nose.

I'll pull my blanket nice and tight,
Arrange my sheets so they're just right.

I'll tuck my animals in just so—
They have their special place, you know.

I'll fluff my pillow for my head
And check one more time under the bed.

Disc Jockey

Most radio stations don't go off the air at night. Running the station, playing music, reading the latest news stories, or answering phone calls are the disc jockeys, or djs. Even at three in the morning, they're on the airwaves, informing and entertaining late-night listeners.

Earth

It's the third planet from the sun, the only one (that we know of) that has life on it, and everyone you know lives there! What is this planet? The Earth. Scientists have learned a lot about the Earth by looking at pictures of it taken from outer space. Because so much of the Earth is water, scientists nicknamed it the Blue Planet.

273

Neptune

The eighth planet from the sun is Neptune. It's dark and very cold there, because it is so far from the sun's heat and light. Neptune is a watery, windy planet. Its winds have been measured at almost 1,300 miles per hour—the fastest winds in our solar system.

Nurse

People sleep in a hospital, but a hospital never sleeps. Nurses who work at a hospital are always on the move, taking care of patients. Some work day shifts and some work at night, bringing patients medicine, changing bandages, taking temperatures, and helping sick people feel more comfortable.

My Toys

They zip and zing
And whir and ring,
They move and talk
Or jump or walk.

My toys can put on quite a show,
They'll zap or whistle, even glow.
My toys are so much fun to play with—
Great to start and end my day with.

My trucks and trolls and electric train
Are always there to entertain.
It's my very favorite way to spend the day;
I just wish my toys put themselves away!

Lunar Ocean

The full moon is bright and pale, but it has many dark patches on its surface. Some are holes called craters. Other spots—large, dark areas on the moon's surface—are places where the surface of the moon is flat. Early scientists thought each of these dark areas was an ocean, and called each one a *mare* (MA-ray), which means "sea" in Latin. There is no water on the moon.

Teddy Bear

Teddy bears are named after the twenty-sixth president of the United States. On a hunting trip in 1906, President Theodore Roosevelt refused to shoot a black bear cub. A cartoon spoofing this story appeared in a newspaper. The cartoon inspired a toy salesman to make a stuffed bear that he nicknamed Teddy's Bear as a joke. It became the most popular toy of the year. Today, all stuffed toy bears are known as teddy bears.

93

Berth

Passengers traveling overnight by train or ship sleep in a special kind of bed called a berth. A berth is a wide shelf covered with a mattress. It folds up into the wall when it's not being used, so it doesn't take up much space on a ship or a train.

Body Asleep, Brain Awake

You're finally relaxed and calm and your body is ready for sleep. As you drift off, your body and mind slow down, but your brain is still at work. It continues to send signals to tell your heart to keep beating, your lungs to keep breathing, your hair, fingernails and toenails to keep growing, and other body parts to keep working.

Charlie Chaplin

Charlie Chaplin was one of the greatest actors and comedians of all time. He was born in England to a very poor family. His mother, a performer, was once singing on stage when she suddenly lost her voice. Only five years old, Charlie was pushed onto the stage, and he started to sing. The audience immediately loved him! Life was not easy, but Charlie worked very hard and eventually became a big success. His movies are loved to this day.

269

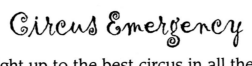

Circus Emergency

"Step right up to the best circus in all the world!" called the ringmaster. Excited, Molly sat in a front row seat, ready to see Trina on the trapeze, Bonita on horseback, Ty and his tigers, and Daisy the clown. The show had just begun when Molly felt a tap on her shoulder. She turned around—it was Daisy the clown! "Sh-h-h," Daisy said, "there's no time to talk. Many of our performers haven't arrived and the show must go on. Please help us!" What do *you* think happened next?

Sagittarius (Archer)

If your birthday is between November 23 and December 21, you are a Sagittarius. This sign is known for a good sense of humor, intelligence, and honesty. Its color is purple. Its gemstone is turquoise. Its animal is the horse. Sagittarius is represented by a centaur—a mythical creature, half human and half horse—shooting an arrow from a bow.

268

Raccoon

At night, this little masked bandit goes out looking for food. Finding food in the dark is easy for raccoons. Their sensitive hands help them find all kinds of good things to eat. Raccoons use their hands to search under bushes, inside holes in trees, and in streams. They even feel around for leftovers in garbage cans! Close your eyes. Can you tell what things are around you just by touching them?

At the Dude Ranch

Would you like to be a cowboy or cowgirl for a day? Imagine that you went to sleep tonight and woke up on a dude ranch. It's a place where you can ride horses and herd cattle on the range. After a day of hard work, you can relax by a warm, crackling campfire with other cowboys and cowgirls, singing songs and telling stories.

Andromeda

In Greek myths, Andromeda is the beautiful daughter of Queen Cassiopeia and King Cepheus. The hero Perseus rescued her from a sea monster. She can be seen best in late winter and early fall.

97

Space Shuttle

6, 5, 4, 3, 2, 1 . . . blastoff! It takes off like a rocket and orbits the Earth. The space shuttle carries astronauts up into space, where they perform experiments, repair telescopes and satellites, and do other projects. Early rockets used to land in the ocean and were never used again. A space shuttle has wings, so it can land on a runway like a plane and can be used over and over again.

Campfire Glow

On a clear, dark night, when you're out in the countryside or the woods, it's fun to gather around a campfire. The crackling, snapping wood, the smell of wood smoke, and the comforting warmth make it a glowing time to sing songs, cook food, and tell stories. Anyone living out in the open, from cowboys on the range to campers in the forest, relies on the heat and light of a campfire.

Kangaroo

A baby kangaroo is called a joey. A newborn joey is tiny—about the size of a bumblebee! Safe in its mother's pouch, it drinks her milk and sleeps until it grows big enough to come out and explore the world. If the joey gets scared, it dives headfirst back into the pouch, then does a somersault and peeks out again, to make sure all is safe.

Cloudscapes

Clouds come in all different shapes and sizes. They are made up of billions of tiny water droplets or ice crystals. Dark, thick clouds mean it will rain. Thin, wispy clouds tell us that the weather is changing. Fluffy white clouds mean it's a beautiful day. Always changing, clouds make pictures in the sky. What picture shapes have you seen in the clouds?

Adaptable Adobe

In the desert, it's hard to keep houses at just the right temperature. The days are sweltering hot and the nights get very cold. A group of Native Americans called the Pueblo once lived in houses made out of thick clay called adobe. Adobe soaks up and holds the sun's heat during the day, keeping the house cool inside. At night, adobe houses are warm, because the clay gives off the heat it has stored.

264

Seaweed

A very useful kind of plant thrives in deep, dark oceans: seaweed. Sea animals such as manatees and all kinds of fish eat it. People eat seaweed, too! It's a healthy ingredient in some kinds of ice cream, cheeses and other foods. In Asian cultures, seaweed is as common a food as green beans and carrots are in the U.S. It's also used in toothpaste and shampoo.

100

Teddy Bear, Teddy Bear

Teddy bear, teddy bear,
Turn around.
Teddy bear, teddy bear,
Touch the ground.
Teddy bear, teddy bear,
Blow out the light.
Teddy bear, teddy bear,
Say good night.

Humpty Dumpty

Humpty Dumpty
Sat on a wall,
Humpty Dumpty
Had a great fall;
All the king's horses
And all the king's men
Couldn't put Humpty together again.

Arctic Lupine

The Arctic is a place near the North Pole that is freezing cold and very dry. The sun shines there only a few months of the year—the rest of the time, it's dark. The plants and flowers have only a short time to grow, bloom, and make new seeds. Since the ground is frozen and hard, the plants can't dig their roots deep, so they spread out wide instead. One Arctic flower, the Arctic lupine, has seed pods that can keep its seeds safe and dry for thousands of years.

262

Bedrock Naps

Is your mattress as hard as a rock? Probably not. Thousands of years ago in Scotland, people actually slept on beds made of stone. But they lined their stone beds with soft moss to help make them more comfortable.

102

Spring Magic

In spring, it's as if the whole world is reborn. Rain falls, trees bud with new leaves and blossoms, flowers bloom, and young plants sprout everywhere. Butterflies, bees, and other insects appear. Animals that have been sleeping through the winter come out of their burrows. The new warmth feels good.
What do you like best about spring?

Giraffe

The world's tallest animal is the giraffe. Giraffes may be tall and strong, but they have to be cautious sleepers. It takes a while for them to bend and fold up their long legs to lie down, and even longer for them to get back on their feet! They take short naps, because they don't want to be caught by their enemies.

Runway Guides

When an airplane gets ready to land at the airport, the pilot can clearly see the airport from miles away, even at night. What helps the pilot see well enough to land the plane? Runway lights. These blue lights line either side of the runway and guide the pilot, showing the right spot for the plane to land. Other lights on the landing field, called approach lights, also help show the pilot where to fly.

Water Spider

The water spider is the only spider that sleeps underwater. It spins a bell-shaped nest that it brings down below the surface of the water. The spider then fills the nest with air bubbles and lives there, sleeps there, and lays its eggs there. It leaves the nest to hunt insects at the water's surface, then brings them underwater to eat.

The Dolphin

*L*egends of many cultures talk about a very small constellation called the Dolphin. Even though it's small, the Dolphin's stars are so close together that it is easily seen on clear, dark nights, especially from July through November.

259

On the Silver Screen

Can you imagine being a movie star? You could ride in a big, long limousine, and wear fancy clothes and costumes. What kind of movie star would you be? Would you like to play the good guy or the bad guy? You'd have to practice signing your name for people when they wanted your autograph. Some movie stars even make up a new name for themselves. Would you call yourself something different just for the movies?

Cricket

Close your eyes and listen carefully. Can you hear crickets chirping outside? You can hear crickets chirping at night almost anywhere, although there are more crickets in the countryside than in the city. Only the male crickets chirp; they make this noise by rubbing their wings together. They do this so that other crickets will hear them and know where they are.

Albert Einstein

As a boy, Einstein was a terrible student. His teachers thought he was not very smart. But he actually was *very* smart—at home, his interest in science was sparked at the age of five, when his father gave him a compass. At twelve, he read his geometry book cover to cover, and began reading more and more complicated books on his own. Eventually, Einstein's ideas about the universe would change the course of science forever.

106

Pablo and Romeo

It happened every single night. Each night, while Pablo lay in bed about to fall asleep, a tiny elf came for a visit. The elf, Romeo, told Pablo wonderful stories all about his home in a land far, far away. But one night when Romeo came, he was carrying a tiny suitcase. "C'mon, Pablo!" said the elf. "Tonight I'm inviting you to visit my home and family. Everything you'll need is in this suitcase. Would you like to come?" What do *you* think happened next?

Words for Bed

*I*n French the word for bed is *lit* (lee), in Spanish it is *cama* (com-ma), in Haitian/Creole it is *cabon* (ka-bann), In Italian it is *letto* (leht-toh), in German it is *bett* (bet) and in Hebrew it is *meta* (mee-tah). But whatever you call it, a bed is still the best place to sleep.

107

Sleepwalking

Some people actually walk around while they're fast asleep. It usually happens when a person is feeling upset or worried. Sometimes members of the same family have this habit. Thankfully, sleepwalkers usually return safely to bed.

256

The Lunar Eclipse

Sometimes the moon moves to the side of the Earth that is facing away from the sun. The moon is gradually covered by the Earth's shadow, until it seems to disappear. This is called a lunar eclipse. People long ago feared the lunar eclipse—some people believed that the moon was being eaten by a dragon, a jaguar, a dog, or even a frog.

Piggy Bank

Do you save your coins by dropping them into a piggy bank? Piggy banks have been used for thousands of years, but they weren't always shaped like pigs. In fact, their name doesn't come from the animal at all! Long ago, some people saved money in jars made of an orange clay called *pygg*.

255

Truck Driver

Throughout the night, truck drivers are on the road, transporting things from place to place. All sorts of things, from cereal to television sets to cars, are delivered during the night, when there are fewer cars on the road. When the trucker gets tired, he stops at a rest area along the highway. Some trucks have a special sleeping area built into the cab, where the driver can stretch out and rest.

How Do Fish Fall Asleep?

How do fish fall asleep
With their eyes wide open in the ocean deep?

What do fish dream about?
Do they dream of schools of famous trout?

How do fish get a drink?
Do they gulp the ocean, or go to a sink?

How do fish stay afloat
Asleep in the sea with no bed and no boat?

Venus

The second planet from the sun, Venus is almost the same size as Earth. Besides the sun and the moon, Venus is the brightest object you can see in the sky. It is called the morning star when it appears at sunrise in the east, and the evening star when it appears at sunset in the west. Venus got its name from the Roman goddess of love and beauty. Who were you named after?

Astronaps

How do astronauts sleep while floating around weightless in the spaceship? Astronauts get to sleep in special sleeping bags that keep them from floating around as they snooze. Spacecrafts have all kinds of equipment on board that help astronauts live comfortably in a place where there's no gravity.

253

Animals, Animals

Animals, animals, I love animals.
The elephant with its very long
  trunk,
The slithery snake, and the stinky
  skunk—
I love the way the lion roars,
How my hamster hurries, and
  when my dog snores.

I love holding kittens in my hand

Or watching crabs walk sideways
  in the sand.
I've brought them all through
  my front door.
Mom says, "Please, no more!"

But when she says it I just laugh,
'Cause outside is my pet giraffe.
Fast or slow, short or tall,
Animals, animals—I love them all.

Mail Carrier

Who brings the mail to your home every day? The mail carrier. Most mail carriers deliver mail on foot, but they also drive mail trucks to help carry large packages. No matter what the weather is—rain or shine, sleet or snow—they bring the mail through. What kind of mail do you like to get in your mailbox?

Silly Putty

Silly Putty was a mistake! Trying to create a new type of rubber, an engineer at the General Electric Company came up with a puzzling new substance: it stretched farther, bounced higher, and lasted longer than rubber. He called it "nutty putty." No one could think of a good use for it until toy-store owner Paul Hodgson thought it would make a great toy. He packaged it in plastic eggs. It was a hit, and has been ever since.

Unchanging Moon

Because of storms, floods, erosion, and other weather, the surface of the Earth has changed a lot over millions of years. Over a long period of time, mountains grow, valleys deepen, rivers widen, and streams dry up. The moon, however, has no atmosphere and no weather to make any changes like these. The moon's surface looks the same today as it always has.

Sleep Years

If you counted all the hours of sleep you had each night, it would add up to a lot of time. Most people average about twenty years of sleep during a lifetime!

Pajamas

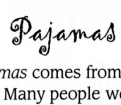

The name *pajamas* comes from the Indian word for "leg clothing." Many people wear pajamas when they go to bed. Pajamas come in many different colors, styles, and materials. There are soft flannel ones for cold nights, and light cotton ones for warm nights. Some even have slippers built in! What are your favorite pajamas?

250

Byron's New Pet

"Now, Leo, don't make a sound," came Byron's voice from outside. What was Byron up to now? Amy, Byron's big sister, wondered. "Byron, help me peel these potatoes!" called Mother. Amy ducked as Byron rushed into the kitchen, then raced back outside minutes later. She crept forward. "Byron, I need the hammer!" Father called. Amy hid again while Byron ran past, then hurried back out. This time, Amy followed. To her amazement, on the back porch stood Byron, leading a huge lion on a leash! What do *you* think happened next?

114

Theodore Roosevelt

When Theodore Roosevelt was a boy, he suffered from asthma. This made him very weak, so he decided to build up his strength. First, he learned how to box. As his strength and his love of the outdoors grew, he went horseback riding and hunting. He grew up to be an explorer, conservationist, soldier, boxer, and the twenty-sixth president of the United States. Did you know that the teddy bear was named after him?

Frog

Have you ever heard frogs croaking at night? They like to sit out in the moist night air and wait for insects to fly by. Then they quickly catch them with their long, sticky tongues. Frogs live in and near water. They move around a lot but will often come back to the same pond over and over again. Sometimes it's the very pond they grew up in.

Scorpio (Scorpion)

*I*f your birthday is between October 24 and
November 22, you are a Scorpio. This sign is known
for strength, excitement, and emotions. Its color is dark
red. Its gemstone is malachite. Its animal is the insect.
In Greek mythology, Scorpio was the name of the
mythical scorpion who fought against
the proud hunter Orion.

248

The Big Dipper

The Big Dipper looks like a big spoon scooping out the darkness of the night sky. It is part of a bigger constellation called Ursa Major, the Great Bear. The two stars at the edge of the bowl point the way to the North Star.

116

Olympic Champion

The Olympic Games are fun and exciting. What would it be like to be an athlete in the Olympics? Which event would you compete in? Would you be nervous? If you tried very hard, practiced a lot, and did your best, you might even win a gold medal! What do you think that would be like?

Traffic-light Talk

One kind of light you see almost every day communicates just by using colors. It's called a traffic light. The red light says, "Stop." The green light says, "Go." The yellow light in the middle means caution or slow down. The first traffic lights were just red and green. Yellow was added later to give people time to slow down.

Light Years Away

Stars are so far away that it takes many years for their light to travel and get close enough to be seen. The twinkling light from a star that is very far away has taken four billion years to reach your eyes. The starlight that you see tonight left those distant stars long before the dinosaurs lived.

246

Windblown

Wind is air in motion. It is created when cool air mixes with warm air. Sometimes wind moves slowly and gently, making a nice breeze. Sometimes it moves very fast and creates a hurricane. The windiest place in the world is Antarctica, where the wind can blow over sixty miles per hour. Wind power can be very helpful—it flies kites, dries clothes, fills sails on sailboats, and drives windmills.

Crocodile

A crocodile spends hours resting in the sun, letting the sun's heat warm its body and help it digest its food. It often naps with its mouth open. Little birds called plovers land on the crocodile's jaw and pick scraps of food out of its teeth. At night, crocodiles sleep floating in the water or resting on muddy riverbanks, with only their eyes and snouts above the surface. They look like logs, which lets them hide from enemies, keep watch for prey, and rest at the same time.

Morning Glories

Morning glories are beautiful flowers that bloom in shades of purple, blue, or white. They wind their way around fences, windows, and archways. Although new blossoms appear early every morning, they only last for one day. When night comes, the blooms all fall off—but there are always more blossoms at sunrise.

119

Longhouse Life

In some countries, one large house, called a longhouse, shelters almost a whole village. Here, relatives and friends of all ages live and sleep in one large room. Platforms separate it into small spaces for each family. The family stores its things under the platform. They make their beds on top of it.

Sleeping Beauty

*O*ne day, a princess decided to climb to the top of a castle tower. There sat an old woman spinning at a spinning wheel. She invited the princess to come closer. The princess touched the spindle of the spinning wheel and pricked her finger. Instantly a spell was cast that made everyone in the castle fall asleep. A hundred years later, a prince entered the sleeping castle, saw the princess, and kissed her. The kiss broke the spell and everyone in the castle awoke.

Sing a Song of Sixpence

Sing a song of sixpence,
A pocket full of rye;
Four and twenty blackbirds,
Baked in a pie.
When the pie was opened,
The birds began to sing;
Wasn't that a dainty dish
To set before the king?

243

Soul Bathing

Taking a bath isn't always just for cleaning your body. People in India who are of the Hindu religion believe that the Ganges River is sacred. During the fall season, thousands of people gather together under the full moon and bathe in the river. For them, it's a bath for the soul.

Planting by the Moon

Many years ago, people decided when and what to plant in their gardens and fields according to the phases of the moon. Some planted during a full moon so the crops would grow well. Other cultures had different ideas. In ancient Rome, some farmers believed that apple trees, olive trees, and grapevines should only be planted when there was no moon in the sky.

Prairie Dog

Prairie dogs live on grasslands and prairies, in underground tunnels and burrows. They dig these "towns" with their sharp front claws. They dig special rooms to sleep in, a nursery for the babies, a separate bathroom, and a secret room where they can sit and listen for danger above the ground.

Tornado Trips

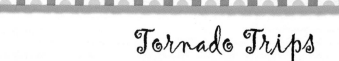

A cool breeze feels nice on a hot day, but when winds pick up speed, they can become very strong! The strongest kind of wind is called a tornado. A tornado is a powerful, swirling wind in the shape of a funnel, blowing over 100 miles per hour. It can pick up and carry anything in its path. Once a jar of pickles was found that had been carried several miles by a tornado, and it wasn't broken! Another tornado swept away a person's important papers in Texas. They were returned by someone over 100 miles away in Oklahoma!

Cave Fish

Cave fish have no eyes. Over the centuries, they have evolved or adapted to living in dark, lightless caves, where they don't need to see. They move about just as sighted fish do, but use their senses of touch and hearing to find their way. Also, because there is no light in a cave, their bodies are very pale in color.

Color Bursts

Up in the sky, on the Fourth of July, brilliant, beautiful fireworks burst and explode. All over the world, fireworks are used to celebrate special holidays. They are made from a mixture of chemicals put inside a paper case. A kind of rocket sends the case up in the air. Then the chemicals inside begin to explode. The different chemicals create different colors: copper creates blue bursts, sodium makes yellow ones, and other chemicals make red, purple, and silver streaks of light.

240

A Time Machine

How would you like to travel back in time? Imagine that you and a friend invented a machine that could send you back to the past, as far as you wanted to go. You'd be the first time-travelers! You would set yourself up in the machine, push all the right buttons, turn on all the right switches, and off you'd go.
Where would you travel to?

124

Pawnee Indians

*T*he Pawnee, one Native American tribe, believed that the stars in the heavens protected people on Earth. The Pawnee had great respect for the stars. To honor them, they arranged their campfires to match the patterns of the constellations they saw in the sky.

Cancer (Crab)

If your birthday is between June 22 and July 22, you are a Cancer. This sign is known for being loving, imaginative, and emotional. Its color is silver gray. Its gemstone is the pearl. Its animal is the crab. Cancer was a crab, a mythological creature who fought against the Greek hero Hercules.

Bat

*I*f it looks like a mouse, but it has wings and can fly, it's a bat! The bat has a special technique for flying and hunting at night, called echolocation. It makes high-pitched cries that bounce off objects, including moths and other insects it likes to eat. The sounds return to the bat and show it where to fly. Bats seem scary, but they're actually very helpful creatures, eating mosquitoes and other pests. Many kinds of bat hang upside down while they sleep.

Queen Victoria

Have you ever imagined that you were a prince or a princess? Over 100 years ago, a little girl named Victoria didn't have to pretend to be royalty—she was! Just like most young girls, Victoria liked to play with her dolls. But as a princess, she also had to study languages, government, music, art, and etiquette (good manners). Victoria was crowned queen of England in 1838, when she was eighteen years old.

126

The Garden

Sandy loved taking care of her garden. One day, she found some new seeds to plant—Wacky Wonder watermelon seeds. "They don't look wacky—they're just plain black seeds!" she thought, but she planted them anyway. That night, she couldn't sleep and got up to look out the window. Sandy could not believe her eyes—in the middle of her garden was a watermelon as big as an elephant! Astonished, she ran outside, looked closely, then gently tapped the giant fruit. "Hello!" a squeaky voice said. What do *you* think happened next?

Quilt

Quilts are blankets that are made by sewing together pieces of different fabrics, making a pattern of many different colors and designs. A quilting bee is a gathering of people to work together on one quilt, each person sewing a different section. The patches of a quilt can be pieces of new cloth, or scraps cut from things like old dresses or shirts.

127

Teeth Count!

When you were a newborn infant, you didn't have any teeth. But you soon grew twenty teeth, which are called your baby teeth. When you grow up, you will have thirty-two adult teeth. How many teeth do you have now?

236

Moon Salute

When astronauts landed on the moon, they proudly stuck an American flag in the ground. In photographs you can see it waving gallantly in the breeze. But it isn't really moving at all. There is no wind on the moon. Wires were put inside the flag to stretch it, making it look as if it's waving in the wind.

128

Dollhouse

Dollhouses can be big or small, simple or fancy. People have enjoyed dollhouses since the 1500s. They were often built for wealthy children as toys or as places to show off other objects. In 1924, Queen Mary had a dollhouse that took four years to build. It had a library of more than two hundred little books, handwritten by famous authors. A New York museum has a dollhouse decorated with miniature paintings by famous artists.

News Reporter

When you are in bed at night fast asleep, things are still going on in the world that will be in the news the next day. News reporters are ready at all times to write about these events. They may get a call in the middle of the night to come to the scene of a fire, to speak to someone in another country, or to fly far away where important things are happening.

Tulips

I know that tulips are from bulbs,
But how come they don't light?

They're purple and they're yellow,
Orange and red and green and white.

And they don't have any lips,
Still they're such a pretty sight,

And these two lips here are my lips,
That will kiss you now good night!

Uranus

Uranus is the seventh planet from the sun. It is named after the ancient Greek god of the heavens. It was discovered "accidentally"—for centuries, people thought Uranus was just another star in the solar system. In fact, William Herschel, the person who first saw it through a telescope, thought Uranus was a comet. But Uranus is a planet, with rings like the planet Saturn and fifteen moons that orbit around it.

Mercury

Mercury is the planet closest to the sun. It's mostly made up of dense rock. Because of Mercury's peculiar orbit, or path, around the sun, a Mercury day is longer than a Mercury year! This small planet was named after the messenger of the mythical Roman gods, because it moves very quickly.

233

Blastoff

Please pack my lunch,
I'm ready to go
Up in a rocket to the moon.
So strap me in and check the
    gears,
Don't worry, I'll be back soon.

Blastoff, liftoff,
Up, up, up,
Way among the stars.

I'll take pictures and send
    you one
From Venus and from Mars.

As I walk on the moon
And collect some rocks
And discover things brand-new,
Take a look up, and you just
    might see
Me waving hello to you!

Police Officer

What would it be like to be a police officer? They work hard around the clock to keep communities safe. A police officer wears a uniform and a bright badge, and carries a special radio that tells her when there is an emergency. When a call comes, she's there to help. A police car or motorcycle flashes bright lights and sounds a loud, shrill siren, letting everyone know that help is on the way.

232

Barbie Doll

$\mathcal{A}$ woman named Ruth Handler invented the Barbie doll. She noticed her daughter Barbie liked to play with paper dolls that looked like adults and had lots of fashionable clothes. Ruth created a doll that looked like a grown-up and had a large wardrobe. She named the doll after her daughter. The Handler's toy company, Mattel, became a huge success when the Barbie doll was introduced in 1958.

Space Underwear

To keep warm in their spaceship, the astronauts wore zipped-up long johns underneath their space suits. On the surface of the moon, though, where it's very hot, they wore special underwear that kept them cool. The underwear was made with tubes attached that were filled with cool water.

Does a Goose Get Goose Bumps?

When you get cold at night, you pull the blankets up to your chin for warmth. Another way your body stays warm is by getting goose bumps. Goose bumps are caused by tiny muscles close to your skin that pull at your hair. When the hair stands on end, it helps trap warm air close to the skin to keep you warm. Geese don't get goose bumps, but monkeys, chimpanzees, and apes do!

133

Trundle Bed

What's a bed under a bed? A trundle bed.
A trundle bed is a single mattress on a collapsible,
wheeled frame. You roll it out from under a regular bed
and it springs up. When you're done sleeping on it, it
folds down and can be rolled back under the
bed until it's needed.

230

Candy Contest

It was a gray, rainy Saturday afternoon. Jenny and Charlie were very bored, so they decided to go to Ollie's Candy Store. They put on their raincoats, grabbed their umbrellas, and left. Just as they arrived at the candy store, bells went off, whistles blew, balloons dropped, and confetti flew. Ollie announced, "Jenny and Charlie, you've got fifteen minutes to take any candy you want, as much as you want, all for free. Ready? Set. Go!" What do *you* think happened next?

Beatrix Potter

$\mathcal{A}$ child of a wealthy family, Beatrix Potter grew up in England. She spent many hours of her childhood reading, drawing, and painting. On family trips to the country, Beatrix liked to draw all kinds of animals and flowers. Once, when she was older, she wrote a letter to a friend's children. In it, she told a story about Flopsy, Mopsy, Cottontail, and Peter Rabbit, and drew pictures of them in the borders. This letter was later published and became the famous *Tale of Peter Rabbit*.

229

Mouse

Mice can live just about everywhere, from houses to fields, and from deserts to grasslands. Most come out only at night to collect food: berries, grass seeds, nuts, and even garbage. A mouse's long front teeth never stop growing, so it's always gnawing and nibbling to keep them worn down to size. What would you do if your front teeth never stopped growing?

135

Bigger and Bigger

Can you imagine what it would be like if you started to grow and grow until you were bigger than the bed, then bigger than this room, then bigger than the house? You could see over rooftops and trees. You could dunk a basketball without any effort at all. You could visit birds in their nests and talk to people in tall buildings. What would it be like to be so big?

The Herdsman

From April through August, look in the night sky for a constellation shaped like an ice-cream cone. This is an easy way to find the Herdsman, whose main star Arcturus is the fourth brightest of all stars and the first star you see after sunset.

Arcturus

Twinkle, Twinkle

Why do stars twinkle? Stars are so far away that they look like tiny dots in the sky. They seem to twinkle because the air moving around us makes the tiny dots appear to shimmer. Planets also shine in the night sky, but they don't twinkle the way stars do. Planets are much closer to us than stars are, so they look bigger, and their appearance isn't affected by moving air. When you see something bright twinkling in the sky, you'll know it's a star. If it shines but doesn't twinkle, it's a planet.

Lighthouse Wonder

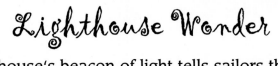

A lighthouse's beacon of light tells sailors that land is near, and warns them of dangerous, rocky shores. The lighthouse keeper used to live in the lighthouse and take care of the lights and the building, but today lighthouses are run with modern equipment, so keepers only have to visit occasionally to check up on things. The tallest lighthouse ever built, the Pharos, was in ancient Egypt. Its light, a large fire, could be seen from thirty miles away on the Mediterranean Sea.

Sea Horse

Sea horses are the slowest-moving fish in the sea. They are unique in another way: the father sea horse gives birth to the babies. After the female lays her eggs in the water, the male gathers them and carries them in a pouch in his belly until they're ready to hatch. When the babies are ready to be born, he releases them into the water.

226

Dinosaur Weather

What was the weather like for the dinosaurs? Millions of years ago, the Earth was covered with large, dense forests and swamps that were hot, muggy, and sticky. The warm climate and moisture allowed many kinds of plants and insects to grow very large. Some kinds of fern were as tall as trees.

Sheltering Huts

People who live in the Kalahari Desert in Africa are always on the move. They follow herds of animals they hunt, such as wildebeest and zebra, or look for water. At night, they sleep on the ground in simple huts made of branches and grass. The women in the group have the job of building the huts—they can construct one in less than an hour.

225

Bulbs

If you want to grow plants, you don't always need seeds. Many flowers, such as daffodils and tulips, grow from something called a bulb. The bulb holds plenty of food for the plant to use when it's planted.
In the fall, gardeners either harvest the bulbs and keep them until next spring when they are replanted, or leave them in the ground through the winter, depending on what kind of bulbs they are.

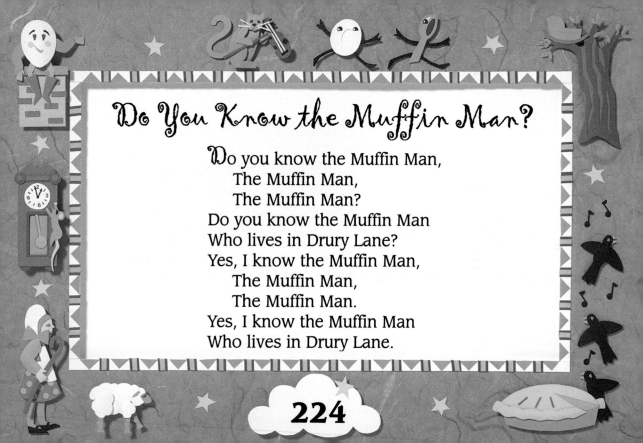

Do You Know the Muffin Man?

Do you know the Muffin Man,
The Muffin Man,
The Muffin Man?
Do you know the Muffin Man
Who lives in Drury Lane?
Yes, I know the Muffin Man,
The Muffin Man,
The Muffin Man.
Yes, I know the Muffin Man
Who lives in Drury Lane.

224

There Was a Crooked Man

There was a crooked man who walked a crooked mile;
He found a crooked sixpence beside a crooked stile.
He bought a crooked cat, which caught a crooked mouse;
And they all lived together in a little crooked house.

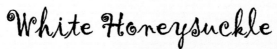

White Honeysuckle

White honeysuckle blossoms have a wonderful scent that fills the air. As night approaches, the scent gets even stronger, attracting night-flying insects such as moths. Bees aren't able to collect the flowers' nectar because it's hard for them to climb inside, but moths can reach inside with their long, strawlike tongues to take a sip.

223

Futon Comfort

*I*f you lived in Japan, you might sleep on a futon. A futon is a mattress, usually filled with cotton or wool and often covered in beautiful fabric. It's firm, but not bouncy like a spring mattress. In Japan, a futon is put on the floor on top of a straw mat called a *tatami*. When not in use, the futon is folded up and stored. In other countries, a futon is placed on a wooden frame that folds up into a couch.

Look for the Rainbow!

You might be lucky enough to see a rainbow if the sun is out during a rain shower. When sunlight shines through falling raindrops, it changes, breaking into different colors. The colors are always in the same order: red, orange, yellow, green, blue, indigo, and violet. Rainbows usually fade away quickly as the rain shower ends or the sun disappears behind clouds. Moonlight can create rainbows, too, but these are rare.

Fish

Fish don't have eyelids so they can't close their eyes. Most fish rest in the water just by slowing down, often at the sandy bottom. One kind of fish, the sole, has both eyes on one side of its head! It spends most of its life on the ocean floor, both eyes facing up.

Light Sight

You need light in order to see. Your eyes work by taking in light and sending signals to your brain, which responds by telling you what you're looking at. The less light there is, the fewer signals the brain gets, and the less you see. Many animals, such as cats, can see much better in the dark than people can—their eyes are better equipped at using every bit of light that's available. Shut off the light and see how many seconds it takes for your eyes to adjust to the darkness.

Youngest Astronaut

Have you ever thought of becoming an astronaut? The youngest astronaut was Gherman S. Titov, a man from the Soviet Union. He was only 25 years old when he went up in the spaceship called Vostok Two. The youngest female astronaut, Valentina Tereshkova, was only 26 years old when she took her first space journey.

143

Cassiopeia
(The Queen)

One of the easiest constellations to find is Cassiopeia, the Queen. The five bright stars form a shape that looks like the letter *W*. The best time to see Cassiopeia is August through March.

Walking, Talking Toys

What if you could make your toys come alive? You could ask them questions and they would answer you. They could give you advice, tell jokes, and play with you all day. You might even use a magic word that they knew was meant just for them—you'd say the word and they'd come alive. Then, if you wanted them to be just regular toys again, you'd say the magic word a second time.

Skunk

With their black-and-white stripes and their powerful smell, skunks are hard to miss! Skunks protect themselves by spraying an attacker with a liquid that smells horrible and stings the eyes. During the day skunks sleep in their dens. At night they roam about looking for their meal of grubs, beetles, and mice.

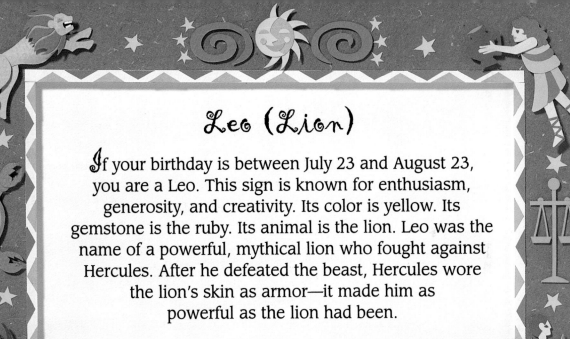

Leo (Lion)

If your birthday is between July 23 and August 23, you are a Leo. This sign is known for enthusiasm, generosity, and creativity. Its color is yellow. Its gemstone is the ruby. Its animal is the lion. Leo was the name of a powerful, mythical lion who fought against Hercules. After he defeated the beast, Hercules wore the lion's skin as armor—it made him as powerful as the lion had been.

The Princess and the Worm

Once there was a beautiful princess who loved animals. But she was sad, because she could never have a pet—she was allergic to them all! Then one morning, after a rainstorm, the princess found a small creature—a worm—lying in a puddle on the sidewalk. He seemed lost, so she took him home. She named him Slimy and kept him in a shallow tank filled with lots of dirt. He was very happy there. But one morning, the princess woke up and found he was gone! What do *you* think happened next?

Wolfgang Amadeus Mozart

Mozart was an amazing musician. When he was only three years old, he began playing the harpsichord. At four, he could already play the violin perfectly and was soon composing his own music. He traveled from town to town with his father and his sister, Nannerl. Both he and his sister played piano for kings, queens, and noblemen. In his lifetime, Mozart wrote over 600 musical pieces. Today, people around the world still play his music.

146

Sleep Stories

Everybody dreams, though many people don't remember their dreams. Some dreams are just a few minutes long, while others can last for an hour. You can have as many as nine dreams in one night! Dreams occur during a period of light sleep called REM, short for rapid eye movement—a time when your eyelids are shut, but your eyes are moving back and forth rapidly, as if you're looking at different things in your dream.

Hammock

What kind of bed swings? A hammock. It's a very simple bed—a wide piece of cloth or woven rope that is tied between two trees or poles. A gently rocking hammock is a very peaceful place to sleep.

Basketball

*H*ow did basketball begin? Dr. James Naismith, who worked at a Massachusetts YMCA, conceived the game in 1891. The players used a soccer ball and peach baskets. As people everywhere started playing the new game, better equipment was created and added. National teams were formed, and basketball was included in the Olympics in 1904. It's now the fastest-growing women's professional sport.

Moon Food

The first astronauts sent to the moon brought specially prepared food. The food was freeze-dried—it was frozen, then all the water was taken out and the food was squeezed into tiny pieces. On the spacecraft, water was added back to the food and it returned to its normal size. Some of the things the astronauts ate were fruit cocktails, sausages, cocoa, bread cubes, and ice cream.

Stuffed-Animal Secrets

There's a bear and a turtle and a dog and a moose,
A rabbit and a monkey and a dolphin and a goose.

All of my stuffed animals surround me in my bed,
They're the only ones that know
The secrets in my head.

Their eyes and ears are falling off,
Their stuffing's out as well—
But they're stuffed with secrets just between us,
And I know they'll never tell.

Air Traffic Controller

High up in a tower at the airport, air traffic controllers stay awake all night, guiding airplanes through the darkness. Air traffic controllers tell pilots how fast to fly and how to navigate through clouds and storms. Special screens show them all the planes around the airport, in the air and on the ground, helping them guide the pilots to safely take off and land.

149

Saturn

Which big planet is known for its bright, wide rings of ice? Saturn. Because Saturn is so far from the sun, it can get as cold as 300 degrees below zero! The second largest planet in our solar system, Saturn doesn't have just one moon like the Earth does— it has at least twenty!

Stars

Like our sun, stars are actually huge balls of brightly burning gas, although they look like dots of light. All stars are very hot. The hottest stars burn white or bluish white, while stars burning at cooler temperatures are yellow and red. Though stars seem very small, if you look carefully you might be able to see what colors they really are.

150

Firefighter

Who can you count on if there's a fire? The firefighters! Firefighters take turns staying overnight at the firehouse. When the alarm rings, they slide down the pole, grab their coats, and hop on the fire truck. The siren roars, red lights flash, and the firefighters are on their way. They climb tall ladders, guide people to safety, and spray water through powerful hoses to put out the flames.

213

Mashed Potatoes

Mashed potatoes,
Smush 'em on the plate.
Mashed potatoes
Always taste so great.
Mashed potatoes,
Make a little mound.
Mashed potatoes,
Pour gravy all around.
Dig 'em, scoop 'em, pat 'em,
Give me a fork and let me at 'em!

151

Mice & Moon

Sometimes the moon looks big and full, sometimes half of it is there, and sometimes it's a tiny sliver. We now know that the moon goes through phases. But there is one Native American legend that says little mice nibble at the moon until it disappears. The moon grows back soon, but only to be eaten away again by the mice a month later.

Slinky

In the early 1940s, an engineer was developing special springs to help ships sail more smoothly on rough seas. One day, he knocked one of these springs off a shelf. It didn't fall all at once, but slowly clumped down from the shelf, coil by coil. His wife thought it would make a great toy and named it the Slinky. Although it never helped sail ships, it has been taken on the space shuttle and used in experiments.

Sizing Up Beds

When Goldilocks tried out the beds of the
three bears, each one was a different size. People's
beds come in different sizes, too. A twin bed is a bed for
one person. A double or full-size bed is a little bigger
and has room for two people. A queen-size bed is bigger
still. And there is the king-size bed, the largest of all.

Give Your Body a Break

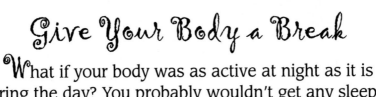

What if your body was as active at night as it is during the day? You probably wouldn't get any sleep at all! Your body slows down during the night to let you get a good rest. Your muscles relax, your appetite goes away, and you can breathe more slowly because you need less air. This way, when you get up in the morning, your body is refreshed and ready to go.

Thomas Edison

As a child, Thomas Edison was always very curious. Once he sat on some goose eggs to see if they would hatch. He experimented with batteries and wires at his home laboratory. When he was twelve, he sold magazines and candy on trains and spent all his earnings on materials for his lab. As an adult, Edison not only invented the lightbulb, motion pictures, and the record player, but he also improved upon other machines, making them easier to use.

No Bath!

Brad didn't like taking baths. He didn't like getting wet and cold and, quite frankly, he enjoyed being dirty. Every night it was the same routine—his mother would try to get him to take a bath, and he'd try to find some way to sneak out of it. Then one night, Brad's mother couldn't believe her eyes. Without being told, Brad went into the bathroom, turned on the water, filled up the tub, got his duck and truck and boat, and closed the door behind him. Tonight, Brad had a secret plan. What do *you* think happened next?

Libra (Scales)

If your birthday is between September 23 and October 23, you are a Libra. This sign is known for being easygoing, sociable, and diplomatic. Its color is any pastel. Its gemstone is opal. Its animal is the lizard. Libra is represented by a pair of scales, which belonged to the Greek goddess of balance and harmony.

Coyote

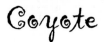

A coyote's tan fur lets it blend in well with its surroundings, but its loud nighttime howl makes it stand out! Scientists aren't sure exactly why coyotes howl, though often it sounds as if they're calling out to each other over long distances. One coyote howls, and soon others join in a coyote chorus that echoes across the night sky. Coyotes are related to dogs and wolves and are very clever animals.

Three Wishes

*I*magine that out there, flying up in the sky, is a magical bird that has very special powers. It would like to share its special powers with you and has decided to grant you three wishes. They can be whatever you want. What would you wish for?

Pegasus
(The Winged Horse)

How would you like to ride a horse with wings? An animal of Greek myths, Pegasus is a beautiful, powerful, winged horse. It is best seen flying through the night sky from August through October.

Deep-sea Glow

The deepest parts of the ocean are very dark. Many of the creatures that live there have special chemicals in their bodies that allow them to create their own light. When it sees danger, the deep-sea starfish begins to glow brightly. This sudden flash of light distracts its enemy, allowing the starfish to escape.

207

Automobile Lights

A car has lots of lights on it, all with different jobs. The headlights in front help the driver see the road in darkness or bad weather. Signal lights on each side blink on and off, telling other drivers that the car is going to turn. Red lights in back shine when the driver uses the brakes, telling other drivers that the car is slowing down or stopping. Police cars, ambulances, and fire trucks have big, colored lights on top that spin and flash in an emergency.

Lion

Most animals in Africa are careful to sleep on their sides or stomachs, so they can be ready to run at the first sign of danger. But lions are lucky. They have no natural enemies, so they can relax. Lions are the only animals in Africa that sleep on their backs. They can just flop over anywhere they like, and start snoring.

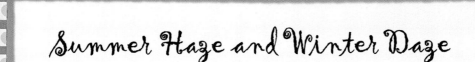

Summer Haze and Winter Daze

Summertime is fun time—the sun is hot and the days are long. There's time to swim, ride bikes, and picnic outside. Wintertime can be fun, too—when there's snow to play in or ice to skate on—but the days are very short. Hot summer temperatures can create thunderstorms, while winter's cold climate can bring about ice storms and blizzards. What other differences are there between these seasons? How are they alike?

Roof Doors

What if your front door was on your roof? People who lived in the ancient Near Eastern city of Catal Huyuk had no streets or sidewalks. Each family went in and out of its house through a door in the roof. Since all their houses were connected, they could easily walk from one home to another. Each living room had benches, built into one of the walls, that were used for sleeping as well as working.

Moonflower

It's dark outside, the moon is out, and all is quiet and still. But not for moonflowers. They are busy opening their fragrant white blossoms in the night air. Found in gardens and meadows, these flowers begin to peek out in the late afternoon and are in full bloom during the night. When morning comes, moonflowers close their petals and go to sleep.

Mary, Mary

Mary, Mary, quite contrary,
How does your garden grow?
With silver bells and cockle shells,
And pretty maids all in a row.

Little Bo-peep

Little Bo-peep
Has lost her sheep
And doesn't know where to find them;
Leave them alone,
And they'll come home,
Wagging their tails behind them.

Bonsai

Bonsai trees are miniature trees or bushes that look like regular trees, but they are only about twelve inches high. Growing bonsai trees is an art that was first developed in Japan centuries ago. Their beautiful, delicate shapes need a lot of trimming and cutting, and they grow best indoors or where there's plenty of shade. Some people have bonsai trees that are over a hundred years old.

Eskimo Nights

The native peoples of the Arctic are called Inuit, or Eskimo. Years ago, each tribe gathered together annually. They met in a big snow house called a *kashim* and spent long hours there, telling stories, singing, and dancing. Parents told stories to their children and grandchildren. Eskimo traditions and culture were passed from generation to generation through the stories told at these gatherings.

The Weather Person

Scientists who are weather experts are called meteorologists. From information collected by weather balloons and satellites high above the Earth, they can tell what the weather is like all over the world. They can even try to predict the weather—though no weather expert is right all the time. The only thing the weather person can be sure of is that the weather is always changing.

202

Wolf

Can you imagine that a wolf, the largest member of the dog family, likes to sleep in a cozy bed just like you do? A wolf makes its own bed by turning around and around in a circle, matting down grass and leaves. It curls up on this grassy cushion and tucks its nose under its tail to keep warm. Wolves live together in large families called packs.

Sunlight

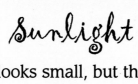

It sometimes looks small, but the sun is really a gigantic star. The sun's light travels very fast—though it's 93 million miles away from the Earth, its light takes only *eight minutes* to reach us! The next closest star is called Alpha Centauri. It takes four years for Alpha Centauri's light to reach Earth!

Milky Way

Our sun and the nine planets we know of make up our solar system. Many, many solar systems—including ours—make up a galaxy called the Milky Way. A galaxy is like a huge community of stars, meteors, planets, moons, and other things. Sometimes you can see part of the Milky Way in the night sky. It looks like a long, faint, white band of light.

Pleiades
(The Seven Sisters)

Seven bright stars that shine very close to one another are known as the Pleiades (plee-a-deez), or Seven Sisters, part of the constellation Taurus. It is really a group of about two hundred stars, though to the naked eye it looks like only seven—or, at first glance, just a small silver cloud. Several Native American myths say they are seven children who wouldn't come to dinner. They kept dancing until they became stars in the sky.

200

Deep in the Sea

What would it be like to be able to swim deep in the sea like a fish? You'd see sunfish, starfish, sea horses, dolphins, and whales. You'd glide and swoop and dive through the water. Maybe you'd come across a sunken treasure chest full of wonderful things. What other things would you see in the sea?

Tokay Gecko

How did tokay geckos get their name? By their call: *"To-kay, to-kay."* These lizards, found in parts of Asia, are often taken in as pets. Tokay geckos are great pets because they eat spiders, insects, and other pests. They scurry around the house all night long, climbing on the walls and even walking on the ceiling! What would you do with a pet gecko?

199

Helen Keller

As an infant, Helen Keller was unable to see, hear, or speak. She couldn't communicate with the rest of the world until she was seven years old, when her teacher, Anne Sullivan, began showing her how to spell and speak using sign language. Helen also learned Braille, a type of writing for the blind, and she typed on a special typewriter. After graduating from college with honors, she spent the rest of her life helping others who also had disabilities.

165

Who'll Play with Morgan?

Morgan was a black-and-white cat who lived on a big farm. Nobody paid much attention to him. He was one of ten cats, three dogs, six horses, and lots of chickens, sheep, and goats. Morgan asked the other animals if they wanted to play with him. But one by one, they each said no. Disappointed, Morgan finally trotted into the henhouse and asked the hens, "Would you like to play with me?" What do *you* think happened next?

Crib

A crib is a bed for babies. It's small and sturdy. The high sides of a crib keep the sleeping baby from falling out. Cribs are often decorated with colorful sheets, bumpers, and musical mobiles.

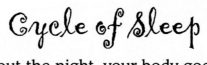

Cycle of Sleep

Throughout the night, your body goes through periods of deep sleep and light sleep. When you're sleeping deeply—usually about a half hour after you first fall asleep—it is very difficult for anyone to wake you up. When you're sleeping lightly, it is easier to be awakened by noise—or someone calling out, "Wake up! You'll be late for school!"

Moon Float

There's no gravity on the moon. So, before they left Earth, astronauts who went to the moon had to practice walking and moving where there was no gravity. How did they do this? They flew in a special plane that swooped and turned, creating moments when the astronauts actually floated around inside. They also practiced underwater, another place where people can float and feel weightless.

Marbles

Adults and children have enjoyed marbles for about five thousand years. The first marbles were made of many materials, from gems to hazelnuts to animal bones. George Washington, Thomas Jefferson, and John Adams all collected marbles, which they called "small bowls." Today, marbles are made of glass. Specific colors and patterns in the glass give the marbles such names as aggies, immies, and peewees. There are over fifty official games that can be played with marbles.

Printing Press Operator

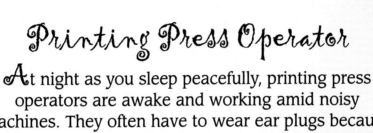

At night as you sleep peacefully, printing press operators are awake and working amid noisy machines. They often have to wear ear plugs because the press is so loud. Printing presses are the big machines that put words and pictures onto paper, for the pages of books, newspapers, and magazines. Printing press operators often work through the night so that newspapers and magazines will be ready for delivery in the morning.

In My Bed

It's the end of another day,
Time to put my cares behind me.
I'll rest my sleepy little head
Upon my warm and cozy bed.
And if you want to find me,
I'll be in dreamland,
Floating, floating
Like a cloud so high.
But still I'm safe and snuggled in
Till the sun is high in the sky.

Comets

A comet is a fantastic sight, with its long, bright tail glowing in the night sky. A comet is made up of frozen gases and ice. As the comet races toward the sun, the sun's heat boils away the ice, creating the huge tail of gas and dust. Comets are usually named for the person who first discovered them. Would you like to have a comet named after you?

169

Northern Lights

$\mathcal{F}$ar, far north, shining in the night sky, are ribbons and swirls of purple, red, and green light. This beautiful sight, called aurora borealis or northern lights, is caused by gases and dust in the air. The northern lights can shine for a few minutes or all night long. They're most visible in Alaska and northern Canada. In the southern hemisphere, they're called aurora australis or southern lights.

Ra's Magic Boat

The ancient Egyptians believed the sun was a god they called Ra. They believed that Ra traveled across the sky during the day in a magic boat, rowed by many strong men. When Ra slept, it became night. The clusters of stars surrounding the North Star were said to be the oarsmen sleeping in the boat.

170

Restaurant Worker

At some diners and restaurants, waiters, waitresses, dishwashers, and cooks work all through the night. Lots of people eat breakfast, lunch, or dinner in the middle of the night: truck drivers, actors in a play, nurses on a night shift, or someone who just wants a midnight snack.

Camel Travel

*I*magine that you need to cross the desert. It's very hot and dry, and you don't have a car. How about a camel ride? With a tasseled blanket and a saddle on its back, the camel is ready for the journey, and you climb aboard. The camel unfolds its long, knobby legs, and stands up. Suddenly you're riding high, over six feet in the air, as the beast crosses the dusty sands.

Golf Balls on the Moon

When astronauts landed on the moon, they had plenty of work to do. They collected rock samples and took pictures of the Earth from outer space. But that's not all they did—Alan Shepard actually played golf on the moon's surface. The ball from Shepard's game is still up there.

Security Guard

At the end of the day, when a store or a museum or a zoo closes, most of the workers go home. But the night security guard's job is just beginning. He wears a uniform and carries a flashlight. The guard patrols the premises all night, making sure everything is safe. When the building opens again in the morning, the security guard goes home to bed.

Night-light

A night-light gives off just enough light to reduce the darkness in a room, without being too bright. When all of the other lights in the room are turned off, the night-light still shines all night long. It is like a personal little light just for you. A night-light can be shaped like many things: a seashell, the moon, or a tiny lightbulb.

Cygnus
(The Swan)

Cygnus is the constellation that looks like a flying swan, with outstretched neck and wings. The stars of Cygnus also form the shape of a cross, so part of this constellation is called the Northern Cross. Look for the Swan in June through November.

173

Babe Ruth

No one knew Babe Ruth's potential when he was a kid. His neighbors thought he would never amount to anything because he was always in trouble. Finally, his parents put him in a reform school when he was eight. There, he played baseball and became the school's star pitcher. He went on to become a huge baseball star, playing for the New York Yankees. When Babe Ruth retired, he had been at bat 8,399 times and had hit 714 home runs, more than any other player before him!

190

The Princess and the Pea

Once there was a prince who couldn't find a princess to marry. One night, he heard a knock at the door. A young woman stood there, needing shelter. "I'm a princess," she told him. The prince didn't believe it, so he decided to test her. Underneath her bed (a stack of twenty mattresses) he put a tiny pea. The next day, she complained that she hadn't slept well because her bed was so bumpy. The prince now knew she had told the truth, because only a real princess could be that sensitive. The prince and princess married soon after.

Virgo (Virgin)

If your birthday is between August 24 and September 22, you are a Virgo. This sign is known for intelligence, order, and reliability. Its colors are gray and brown. Its gemstone is agate. Its animals are the cat and dog. In Greek myths, Virgo was the daughter of Demeter, goddess of nature and the seasons of the year.

Three Wishes

As I was walking down the street
I saw a teeny little man
No bigger than my little toe.
He said, "Please help me if you can."

He said he had three wishes
That he had to give away,
And if I took him home with me,
It would be my lucky day.

So I put him in my pocket
And he still stays with me,
But I'm still trying to make up my mind
What my three wishes are going to be.

175

A Terrific Train Ride

Close your eyes and imagine yourself riding on a train. Feel the gentle rumble of the train along the tracks, and hear the *toot-toot* of the whistle. Some trains have a dining car and serve fancy food. Some have sleeping compartments where you can sleep while taking an overnight trip. Trains go over bridges, through tunnels, around mountains, and through valleys. Where would you like the train to take you?

188

Ten Pins

Did you know that many years ago in the United States you could get arrested for bowling? In Colonial America, bowling was against the law because bets were placed on it. At that time, the game was called nine pins, and the object of the game was to knock nine pins over by rolling a ball into them. Since the law banned only nine-pin bowling, people added an extra pin, making it a game of ten pins, which was no longer against the law! Now known as bowling, ten pins is played to this day.

Stardust

Sometimes stars far out in space explode and their pieces scatter. These pieces are called stardust. Pieces of stardust can be as tiny as house dust or as big as stones. Sometimes the dust lands on other planets, or forms new ones. The Earth picks up more than a thousand tons of stardust each day!

187

Sleep Moving

Did you know that as you sleep, your body doesn't stay still? While you are asleep, you move to change positions, to pull your blanket closer when you are cold, to push the covers off when you are too hot, or to move an arm or a leg to get comfortable. Most people move about every ten minutes in their sleep. You may move about in bed like this fifty times in one night, all without ever waking up!

Horse

Do you think you could fall asleep standing up?
Horses can do it without any problem—when they
relax, their legs lock in place. Horses like to rest or
sleep standing up, because it's more comfortable for
them than lying down. Sometimes a pair of horses will
rest together. They stand side by side but face different
directions, each horse's tail swishing to keep
the flies off the other's face.

186

Mysterious Message

"**Y**ay! We're finally at the beach," said Ray. "Let's go walk along the sand and collect shells," said his sister, Anna. They found many beautiful blue, white, and orange ones. Then something caught Ray's eye. He saw a large bottle lying in the sand and picked it up. "Look," said Anna, "there's a piece of paper inside." Ray reached into the bottle and took out a crumpled note. He and Anna opened it and began to read the first line. What do *you* think happened next?

Bird's Nest Soup

In Malaysia, thousands of birds called swiftlets use their saliva to build nests high atop the walls of dark, damp caves. The local people love to eat the nests. After the swiftlet chicks have hatched and flown away, the people climb tall bamboo ladders and collect the old nests. From this harvest, they make a dish called bird's nest soup. They clean the nests and boil them in thick chicken stock.

Opossum

When an opossum needs to fool other animals, it lies very still and doesn't move. The other animals think the opossum is dead and leave it alone. This trick is called playing possum. Like kangaroos, opossums are marsupials—they carry their babies in a pouch. They are the only pouched animals in North America.

179

This Little Piggie

This little piggie went to market,
This little piggie stayed home,
This little piggie had roast beef,
And this little piggie had none,
And this little piggie cried wee-wee-wee
All the way home.

The Arrow

Who shot the Arrow up into the air? There are many stories about this constellation. Some say Hercules, some say it belonged to Apollo, and some say it was one of Cupid's arrows of love. Look for it from July through November.

180

Evergreens

Have you ever noticed that during the coldest part of the year, many trees have no leaves while others stay green? The green trees are called evergreens. They have needles instead of leaves. Evergreens are good friends to birds and animals because their branches and thick needles provide shelter during snowstorms. Do you know if there are any evergreens in your neighborhood?

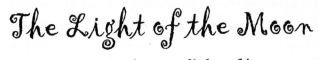

The Light of the Moon

The moon doesn't make any light of its own—it gets its light from the sun. The sun shines on the surface of the moon and is reflected back. The other side of the moon remains in shadow. When you see a half-moon or crescent moon, look carefully—you may be able to see the dark side of the moon as well.

181

Where Is the Lightning?

A hot summer night can bring electrical storms—lightning flashes across the sky and thunder roars. Lightning is electricity, the same kind of energy that makes the lights in your house work. Thunder is the sound of hot air moving. It's easy to figure out how far away lightning is: When lightning flashes, count the seconds until you hear the thunder rumble. For every five seconds, there's one mile between you and the lightning.

182